The Wrinkle Ranch

To Boz!

Peace & Love
to you, your family
& friends ♥

Mercy Kennedy McCallister

Stowe, Vermont

2015

The Wrinkle Ranch

A Novel

By Mercy Kennedy McAllister

The Wrinkle Ranch

A NOVEL

LCCN - 2015901773
ISBN – (13 digit) 978-0-692-38210-3
Printed in the United States of America by
CreateSpace, an Amazon.com company

Photography courtesy of Maralena J. Stevens

MKM Novels
P.O. Box 85
Craftsbury, Vermont 05826

mkm.thewrinkleranch@gmail.com
www.mkmnovelsthewrinkleranch.com

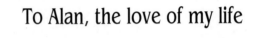
To Alan, the love of my life

In my constant thoughts:

Det. Sgt. Patrick K. & Margaret K.
Cass & Joe K. (WWII)
Marie & Dutch
Alice & Al
Katherine & Bill (WWII)
Tricia & Ernie
Ann & Dewey (WWII)
Pat (Navy Veteran) & Pat
Mary Ellen & Ferd (WWII)
Albina & Phil
Jack (WWII) & Jean
Ernie (WWII) & Janet

*My heartfelt thanks to Nancy H., Courtney B. and Coreen F.,
for sharing their valuable time, energy and support.*

One of the most wonderful times of my life took place between the years of 1966 and 1969, when our friends and I, along with my husband, lived under one roof. Some people called it a commune, but we called it "Peaceful", an old house along the Russian River north of San Francisco, built during the gold rush. We lived there rent free. The owner furnished the materials and we did the labor. That was the deal. Even after renovations, it wasn't beautiful, but the journey was priceless.

The 60's was a time of transition, from a period when people were preoccupied with status and being told how to live, while feeling a constant pull of how they wanted to live.
While sharing what we had, each bringing our own possessions, skills and resources, we took care of each other and created memories to last us a lifetime.

It was a time of yearning, when some of us were estranged and searching for a home. It was a time of understanding, to know and accept people outside of our traditional and often times isolated families. Where there was pain, we infused love. Where there was uncertainty, we added hope.

During those years we learned about love, compassion and sustenance. We learned, through patience and tolerance, about people different from ourselves in culture, thoughts, and personalities; that everyone should be accepted and respected for who they were. There was no grandiosity. No one individual had the answer for everything.

As children growing up we all watched the same television shows and naively believed that everyone lived in pretty houses overflowing with a loving family, doing chores without complaining. This is what we had in mind, I think, when we met in Golden Gate Park, in search of peace and love; something we could call our own.

I'd like to think that the time we spent together helped set the tone for how we lived our future lives. Perhaps I held a utopian view of those years, but I do believe that in one brief span of time, we thrived in peaceful surroundings while existing in a much larger tumultuous world. For a few, it would turn out to be the only peace they had ever known.

All things do pass eventually and we did move on, some seeking a more traditional lifestyle back east, others going on to graduate or law school. Some were sent to Vietnam or took refuge in Canada. Like a family ripped apart by death or divorce, we dispersed and lost touch.

After Tom passed away, I sold our home in northern Minnesota and reluctantly moved in with my son and his wife; an icy reminder to never trust anyone over the age of thirty.

I can't really say I was in search of a new life, only that I had been forced to start another. I was always one of those people who were at their best going against a headwind and where none existed, created one; or like a sled dog trained to pull, rarely slowing down.

Downsizing was challenging, but eventually my possessions were whittled down to fit into a large bedroom that was not my own. An almost palpable tension in the house made me feel like an unwanted guest.

In thinking about my future, I found myself reliving my past. Here I was living in a home that wasn't mine, in a town not by my choosing; feeling restless like an adolescent, when all I wanted to do was dance.

An annoyance plagued me that I'd never get to do the things I wanted, like climb Kilimanjaro or kayak the Inside Passage, lofty goals for someone who hasn't stretched since 1973.

I became painfully aware that in the near future I'd need to relinquish driving altogether and live within these walls, with a cat I didn't like and a daughter-in-law who smelled.

Over the next few days I watched news reports about the shortage of living options facing aging baby boomers, millions of Americans born between 1946 and 1964. They called it the 2030 problem, when there'd be nearly 74 million boomers over the age of 65.

What *were* our parents thinking?

The reports talked of shortages in assisted living apartments, group homes and beds in places where people received skilled nursing care. Most of the boomers, living healthier longer, didn't meet the medical requirements for nursing care. Those sandwiched in the middle, like me, needing some help, but not a lot, could go to a group home, if they could find one. Some boomers never married or had children and everyone required their own individual living plan to meet their own needs.

Applications to open new group homes skyrocketed, and most states couldn't meet the staffing demands required to inspect homes nor do background checks on caretakers. Back logs tripled and nursing homes couldn't be built fast enough to meet the rush of humanity barreling toward their doors.

Reports told of others, who preferred to stay in their own homes, but no funding was available to pay for services, like personal care attendants, to help support that plan. In some places, existing services were booked solid for over a year.

After decades of marriage, couples were sent to separate nursing homes in different states. There was a family get- together, along with a big cake; photos were taken of them saying good-bye to each other - sort of like a reverse wedding. Stories like this echoed around the country.

The reports concluded that the government would create a task force to look into the matter, that Congress would approve more funds. Experts gave their opinions, offering few solutions.

While listening to these reports I realized they were talking about me. I was one of those aging baby boomers. My house was gone and I was living with my son and his wife. The plan sounded like a good idea at first, with plenty of cash and good health, my future had looked bright. But now here I was, with one foot in the rabbit hole.

I continued to ask myself the same question. Is this where I want to live out the remaining, possibly 25, years of my one and only life?

More importantly, was it necessary to be so dependent on *her* when no longer able to drive? Would she need to know when I bought diapers or if I just wanted to browse the make-up aisle or buy junk jewelry? Would she watch the clock impatiently, arm akimbo, rushing me about for taking too long?

I'd be tethered to her side like a child, going places only when *she* could take me and only when her calendar was clear. *She* was free most nights, except Thursdays, when she went to quilting class. That's where she said she was going, but I never believed her.

So, here I was asking all the right questions, but answers were elusive. Feeling trapped in a way I never felt before, thoughts about Peaceful entered my mind and the contentedness we all felt there.

What ingredients were used to bake that magic? Where were my friends now? Are they being cared for by people who love them, or are they sick, scared and alone? Are we still on the same planet?

Struggling to find a new place in this world with a body difficult to steer was challenging and so facing a headwind once again, I steeled myself to search for the answers. I decided to embark upon a journey to find the party, where acceptance awaited me and music invited my body to move with grace.

Without too much trouble I located Carolyn living in a small community west of Tucson, Arizona. It turned out that she too was a widow and living in a spacious three bedroom home. Some of her angst involved the upkeep of landscaping around her home and while there was no lawn to mow, she did have grapefruit trees to harvest. This was challenging as she suffered from arthritis.

The concept of growing grapefruit in your own backyard was a new one to me and I thought it simply magical. Overdue for much needed sunshine, I packed my bags and headed to the southwest, a place I longed to visit.

Of all the friends in the crowd, Carolyn was the most special. She was wise beyond her years and had a sweet unassuming nature about her. A never-ending sorrow remained in our hearts for the pain Carolyn endured after losing Roger, her true love, to a mortar round in a jungle on the other side of the world.

I was surprised to see a short rounded body hugging the doorway, such a contrast to my memory of her leggy frame. And while here she was all anew, her eyes still held that mixture of wisdom sprinkled with joy and her wide smile gave me a feeling of renewed comfort.

"So, how is it that you still look so beautiful after all these years?" I asked with open arms.

"I think it's the sun. I wish I felt beautiful. All this week I had to use a walker because of back pain. Let's sit ...tell me more about your life with the doctor," Carolyn said as we walked inside her home where everything was white.

As she spoke Carolyn removed the contents of a small ceramic canister and proceeded to roll a joint. She turned to me and smiled brightly: "Medical marijuana...for my pain."
We added some music and rested shoulder to shoulder while I babbled on about the doctor, the conventional banquets and our vagabond lifestyle crisscrossing the country.

It all felt so familiar, as if we had never missed a beat.

So there we were, transported back in time, sitting on the couch stoned. The air was hot, but it was a dry heat, and the cloudless sky afforded me a gift of yellow light I never saw before. The brightness stretched into infinity.

While chatting vigorously we dined alfresco on fruit, vegetables and chips. I sensed that this was most likely her place of comfort, outside under the covered lanai, in a padded reclining chair surrounded by lush gardens that held roses, succulents, red and purple bougainvillea and towering palms.

The sides and rear of the house, surrounded by high concrete walls painted mauve pink, offered much privacy and a runway for a flock of spying quail. The last time I saw quail was at the opposite end of my fork.

This place was such a contrast to the life I lived, but as close to paradise as one could be. We talked long into the night until Carolyn fell asleep on the living room couch.

It didn't take long for me to notice that Carolyn was struggling to live in the house alone. Her bedroom, on the second floor, made sleeping on the couch routine. She asked me to fetch mail at the end of her driveway, a trip she rarely made and she didn't drive much, preferring to use a taxi for errands or doctor visits. Groceries were delivered by a service that charged a percentage of the bill, payable in cash, and food orders were small, resulting in inadequate food storage and repeated orders.

It had been a while since her house was cleaned. The throw rugs were stored inside the washer and dryer, not used in over a year. Home health aides visited weekly helping Carolyn to shower, each week a different person, male or female entered her home. She opened the door to anyone who knocked, choosing to live a life without fear.

Understanding Carolyn's wishes to age while living in the privacy of her home, did not dismiss my growing concern. As a retired emergency room nurse, I had hardened over the years and at times felt like a borderline misanthropist, an affliction that kept me safe.

I learned that Carolyn was estranged from her only son, Jackson living in England, who hadn't called or visited for over five years. Jackson was the only child born to Roger and Carolyn and she had raised him alone up to the age of ten when she married Harold, of whom she rarely spoke.

Carolyn learned early that Jackson was gifted and at the age of thirteen enrolled him in an education program in England where he remained into adulthood. There had been tension between Jackson and Harold that went unresolved, a topic that was off limits.

"Why don't I see more people walking around? The town looks deserted."

"Most people here are either early retirees or the extreme elderly. Those that can get out either play golf or go shopping - those that can't, stay indoors. You won't see a lot of people walking in the hot sun. Errands are done first thing, while the air is cool," she replied.

"And why am I so hot?"

As a long term resident of northern climates, I was sweating profusely inside Carolyn's air conditioned house.

"That's because my air conditioner is set at 87, a higher temperature number than you need for cooler air. We can turn it down to make it cooler for you, but then I might freeze to death. Let's see if we can find a good middle ground," Carolyn replied.

We talked about the extreme hot weather in summer, its effect on the body, the sand storms, scorpions and the coyotes that roamed the streets all hours of the day.

We talked about how the taxi driver took her to the bank, then to the doctor, then to the marijuana dispensary and then back to her house, where he knew she was alone and had cash.

Had I become so distrustful that I could no longer see beauty in the world? What metaphysical presence intervened bringing my skeptic eyes to Carolyn in her time of need? I'd soon find out.

Before leaving for Minnesota, Carolyn and I made changes. We stocked her freezer and cabinets full of food, hired a handyman to move her bedroom to the first floor, did laundry, arranged for the postal service to deliver mail to the door and arranged for a pharmacy to deliver her pills.

The personal care attendant scheduled visits in advance and Carolyn's neighbor would visit on those days so that she was not alone in the house with a stranger. We made arrangements for her physician to do home visits and scheduled physical therapy at a local pool that offered free transportation.

And finally, with great sadness we arranged to have the grapefruit trees cut down, replacing them with two flowering cacti. We agreed to talk every Wednesday at 2pm and I left Arizona feeling good about the safety of my friend.

When I returned, it was no surprise that I landed in a dark Minnesota and entered a chilly house. Remaining in my room until dinner, my son approached with what he thought was a solution to his problem. How I birthed this right wing bureaucrat from my free spirited body will always remain a mystery to me.

Without batting an eye he told me I'd be visiting assisted living places by week's end; that the social and recreational opportunities were in my best interest. The monthly costs were steep.

"What if I don't want to spend my money to live in a place like that?" I asked sternly.

"There are less costly arrangements, like living in a house with a neighbor," he added.

"Have you seen the reports? There are waiting lists," I replied. We locked horns.

Knowing exactly what they were up to, I didn't give in as easily as they had hoped. Did they not see that I could see *his* eyes meet with *hers* across the table when I spoke? Are they really that dense or do they mistakenly believe I'm no longer the sharpest pencil in the box? Do they believe I'm empty and dry like the sheath of a snake's skin, devoid of all feeling?

Uncertainty engulfed me, but no matter how they sexed it up, no part of me was ready to spend my days surrounded by broken bodies, engaging in banal conversation or being herded onto the short bus for day trips to the zoo.

Carolyn was adamant about living in her home as long as possible. I, on the other hand, was homeless. It was clear I couldn't maintain a home bigger than a condo and in due time, being unable to drive, that plan too would sour.

Who wants to live in a condo all by themselves? Maybe I could get a little dog or a couple of fish. I felt as though I was on an island between two worlds, too healthy for a nursing home, yet too fragile to scurry about without help to do things like driving and shopping alone.

Maybe assisted living was the right choice, but not for me, not yet. I planned to hatch a different scheme altogether – one that puts me at the helm in charge of my own destiny; a final journey in search of a contentedness I hadn't felt in a long, long time.

It was Wednesday and after several attempts Carolyn didn't pick up the phone. Growing nervous, I asked a neighbor to check on her; he had a key, so I asked him to use it.

He found the front door ajar and the day's mail was strewn about inside the hallway. He found Carolyn in the kitchen, there was blood; police were on their way.

"I'm leaving for Arizona and don't know when I'll be back," I said to my son.

"So, you're going to stay with that old hippie friend of yours?" he barked.

"I'm not interested in living with strangers and I'm too healthy for a nursing home. I feel great and besides, I'm concerned about my friend, whom I loved long before you were born. I'll give you a call when I get settled," I said while getting in the taxi.

Was I so invisible that he saw nothing when looking into my eyes? When did I cease being an individual and when did I relinquish control of my life?

Life was so strange. Here I had all the money I could ever want, yet homeless and without a plan. I cursed Tom for leaving me alone. How dare he not tell me about his heart condition.

Carolyn had been sent home from the emergency room by the time I arrived. She suffered from a gash in the back of her head when hitting the tiled floor.

Earlier that day she called the taxi to go to the bank and then to the dispensary to pick up her prescription for marijuana. The police think she was followed because shortly after the taxi dropped her off, a man knocked at the door saying he was there to do a maintenance check on her air conditioner.

When she refused to let him in, he pushed her hard and demanded to know where she kept her cash and drugs.

When Carolyn fell to the floor, she activated the emergency button on her wrist and within seconds a voice came over the intercom. Was she injured? Did she need assistance?

Knowing they would send police if she didn't respond, she remained quiet. The intercom scared off her assailant, but not before he stole cash and all prescription drugs, including the weed.

"I'm surprised you came all the way back here for me," Carolyn said as she rested in the lounge chair eyeballing the luggage. "Did you remember to take the silver?" she joked.

"If you don't mind, I'd like to stay for a while. With Tom gone, there's nothing for me in Minnesota. My son wants me to move into assisted living," I said while massaging her feet.

"Funny you mentioned that. Nurses at the hospital were talking about a shortage of places available…long waiting lists. Why don't you stay here and we can take care of each other?" Carolyn said with her eyes opened wider than I had seen them all day.

Moments later I noticed a police officer about to knock at the door. They had received a call from a woman in England by the name of Francine. It was about Jackson. Their job today was to do a death notification. Jackson was found dead while on vacation in Paris.

Jackson's remains were cremated and due to arrive at the house tomorrow. Carolyn never heard of Francine, but police said it sounded as if she was a member of the family.

The next day, a box containing Jackson's cremated remains arrived from Paris as promised. There was a formal but brief letter sent by authorities outlining the circumstances as they understood them to be. He was alone in the hotel when he died and cause of death was an apparent heart attack.

Jackson was just 45 years old with no known health problems. Foul play was not suspected.

The scene was too familiar. In much the same way, over four decades ago, she was informed that Roger had been killed in Vietnam.

All of the men in her life were gone and our endearing lady felt very much alone. Was it Jackson who sent me to Carolyn's side?

After reminding myself that life is short and not always fair, my decision to stay in Arizona was made. A memorial service would be held in two weeks for Jackson and I hoped this was all the time I'd need to gather those who were present when he was brought into this world.

I asked a neighbor to help me find our friends. I was able to find Doug and Sumana, who were still married and living in New Hampshire. They had one daughter whom they had not seen for quite some time. Doug was a retired government worker and Sumana was a retired social worker who was also an artist.

We found Mitch, a retired Paramedic, living in the Northwest part of the country close to the Canadian border. He was single and had two grown sons from a prior marriage. Mitch was able to locate Gary, who we learned was a lawyer still practicing in northern California. Gary was also single, but had never married. They all planned to attend the memorial service and agreed this would be a surprise for Carolyn.

Of all the people I had hoped to find, was Philip. I knew he'd want to be here for Carolyn, as Philip was close to Roger and took his death hard. After receiving his draft notice, Philip left Peaceful in the dark of the night without saying good-bye. We all presumed he went to Canada, but never knew for sure.

After a few days our mood softened, and I approached Carolyn about an idea. For security reasons, I wanted to add some noise makers to the household – those being two miniature Chihuahuas. Carolyn loved the idea and our new roommates, "Thunder" and "Rocket" delightfully entered the picture. They were easy to pick up and required only short walks. The backyard was their playground and both used their own litter box inside. Their barking let us know when anyone came to the door and while concerned we might sit on them, I concluded that as long as we provided food, water and shelter, it was their job to avoid injury and stay off the couch.

In the days before the memorial Carolyn submitted a long and beautiful obituary for Jackson to several California and Arizona newspapers. If Philip was on the west coast, he'd see it.

"I don't even know why I'm having this service. Who will come? No one knew him in this area," she said sounding nervous. "And who is this Francine woman?"

I reminded her that memorial services were for the living, that there'd likely be people who knew her and Harold who'd want to pay their respects.

"Actually, I think everyone is dead," she added.

"Not everyone is dead," I replied. "You'd be surprised who might show up," I said reassuringly.

My thoughts turned once again to Philip. Our relationship ended before I married Tom, but I often wondered how my life would've turned out if we'd stayed together. Philip was always designing and building things; a resourceful scavenger. Philip and Tom were so different, they could never really see eye to eye when it came to me.

Tom had a jealous streak and breathed a sigh of relief when Philip turned up missing. But even though my thoughts returned to Philip from time to time, my heart belonged to Tom - except for that one last night, when Philip asked me to meet him down by the river.

That was the week I got pregnant.

As promised, they all arrived at the memorial service. Carolyn was overwhelmed with emotion and we watched as her eyes overflowed with a lifetime of tears. To her surprise there were many in attendance and her heart found peace.

When the service was drawing to a close, a tall robust man wearing a hat searched the room before entering. He appeared awkward and hesitant, uncertain if he belonged. For a moment, I thought it was my son. But instead, I saw that it was Philip. Until that moment, it had never occurred to me. The resemblance was uncanny.

When Philip's draft number was called up, he flew back to New York to say good-bye to his parents, with every intention of going to Canada. He spent two weeks living in the woods of northern Vermont only to turn around at the border, not yet ready to give up on his country.

He did two tours in Vietnam and was hospitalized upon returning to the states. Describing himself as a "homeless lost soul" living on the streets of Los Angeles, he changed his name and later emerged a rag's to riches story working as an architect. Philip started his own firm designing buildings in Los Angeles, Mexico and Las Vegas. He never married or had children, but spent the last 20 years with a woman who has since passed away.

When asked why he changed his name, he said that his father had been involved in some shady stock market business back east and he wanted to sever ties.

Following the memorial service, we returned to Carolyn's to reflect on the day. We sunk into the comfortable white leather couches and listened as we each talked about our lives.

Doug and Sumana planned to move to the southwest and were estranged from their only daughter who left town with a man they didn't like.

Mitch reported that he wore two hearing aids and could still hear the sirens from his rescue vehicle. He added that he didn't have much of a life in the city; that he was just renting and looking to make a change.

When it was Gary's turn, he looked up slowly and in a familiar soft voice stated, "I have no family....but I do have stage IV prostate cancer." We all looked downward without speaking, and for some reason I sensed that we felt just a little older.

When it was my turn I explained how my son was growling at me to move into an assisted living place.

"Good luck finding one. There's a shortage due to the baby boomer's aging out," Philip stated showing a look of concern on his face.

"I heard there were waiting lists; they can't build them fast enough," Sumana added.

"Patients will be stacked up in hospital hallways to get the care they need," I added.

"We'll need to go back to the ways of the past, where family took care of each other to the end," stated Gary.

Then Carolyn explained that I had moved in with her, that we were going to take care of each other as long as we could.

"We have more money than we ever had. I own the house, and there are tons of things to do around here: restaurants, shopping and health care facilities. And, most importantly, we have Thunder and Rocket to protect us. Who could ask for more?" she added. Everyone laughed but this could not lift the mood or growing concern over Gary's announcement.

I introduced the concept of caring for each other right here, right now, that Carolyn had two more bedrooms to fill. Curious, I asked the others what they wanted, what was their end of life plan?

"I want to spend the rest of my life in sunshine with people I know," replied Doug. "This past winter was just too cold."

"Me too," added Sumana as she threaded her arm through Doug's. "I'm afraid I'll slip on the ice."

"Right now all I can think about is the cancer – I want to treat it the best way I can. I'm sure I'd be happy with the care I got in Arizona," reasoned Gary.

"I want to try and lose some weight. I'm a heart attack waiting to happen. Other than some business and a house falling into the ocean, there's nothing holding me to California," Philip said quietly looking down at his strong broad hands that looked very familiar to me.

"I'd like to avoid going to a sterile environment where I don't know anyone," added Sumana.

"I'd like to wake up and not hear sirens. It seems a lot quieter around here. I don't sleep well when the only voice I hear is my own," Mitch added turning to Carolyn.

"I don't want to be alone. I have the best neighbors anyone could want, but in all fairness, you can only rely on them so much," stated Carolyn. "With my arthritis, I have good days, bad days and then *very* bad days. What are your thoughts, Sharon?" Carolyn asked turning to me.

"I've been asking myself that question and I'm not sure I'll ever have the perfect answer. When did moving into assisted living become a normal phase in the aging process? Now, it seems as if it's something we *must* do, in the natural order of things, like going to college."

"I like living in the sun, eating good food, drinking good wine, caring for my friends and dancing to music. I want good health care and to be safe."

"I don't want to be alone either, but I'm not yet ready to be herded as part of a group simply for the convenience of the caretaker."

"I like the idea of living with people who know who I am, where I came from and the people in my thoughts and heart like Tom, John, Roger, Jackson and all of you. I like the idea of living with people who remember that I was once beautiful, wore flowers in my hair, danced half naked on the beach and skinny dipped in the river. Would it be such a bad idea for us to come together as we did before? We'll never know unless we try," I concluded.

Everyone agreed right off that this was as good a plan as any and as a certain excitement took hold they all went back home to settle their personal affairs, to return over the next few weeks. Our immediate concern was Gary's health.

Before leaving he shared his worst nightmare with me: "If I fell dead in the street, there'd be no one to call to claim my cold lifeless body." The same held true for Carolyn had I not entered the picture, and this convinced me even further that our plan made sense. The time was right.

Later that night Carolyn pulled me aside quietly.

"Sharon, I need to ask you something. I couldn't help notice the striking resemblance between Philip and the photos you showed me of your son. Is this just a coincidence?"

"I'm not sure," was all I could say.

Was it truly possible that Philip could be John's father? As a nurse I knew that answer, but as a mother and wife of John's now deceased thought-to-be father, I question which part of this web needed to be untangled this late in the game. If fate has dealt me this blow, then fate will need to fix it, and I thought it best to say nothing for now.

Carolyn and I talked long into the night. We talked about our parents and how different their lives were compared to ours; how it was commonplace for most families to care for their aging parents and grandparents at home until the very end - long before the time when warehousing our elderly turned into a multibillion dollar industry.

Carolyn's father had served in WWII as a Paratrooper. In December of 1944 his unit fought in the Battle of the Bulge and he was nearly captured as he hid beneath a disabled Panzer in the snow covered frozen terrain, as German soldiers searched the surrounding woods. His hands and feet suffered from frostbite, but he survived.

Roger's father served on the USS Lexington, a carrier in the Pacific theatre attacked by the Japanese. The men had to abandon ship and were later rescued.

Those who served our country in WWII were everyday people thrust into circumstances beyond belief. They were men and women who stepped forward willingly or were drafted, sacrificing either life or limb or a piece of their soul to fight against tyranny. We wouldn't have the life we have today if it wasn't for their valiant fight for freedom.

To think of it all left us emotionally overwhelmed with heavy hearts, in part because of how proud we were of their courage and in part because of the sadness we felt for those who were imprisoned, tortured or lost their lives.

We talked long into the night about their legacy and it gave us great comfort to know that we were the first children born to that great generation. Rising from this influence, we too went on to accomplish great things. They quietly passed to us a fist full of strength that helped to raise our awareness and lend our voices to the cries for equality, cries against injustice and inequity and the fight for civil rights. We helped put an end to an unpopular war and ignited a social and cultural revolution that helped spur the creation of some of the most powerful music ever created upon this earth. Like an unending chain reaction, their legacy lives on.

Carolyn and I felt good about our plans.

There was a familiar cohesiveness between all of us at the end of the day. And there seemed to be a silent promise, a reassurance that everything would be okay.

Maybe it was because we believed in each other and had hope or perhaps it was a simple desire to know each other again and to live together like families did in the past - like we did at Peaceful.

Similar to a marriage, this was a permanent exercise in commitment, yet a calm ambiance existed, as if it was all meant to be. Perhaps we knew that in sharing the responsibility among us we'd find strength in numbers once again.

Or perhaps we were comforted to know we had a place to live out the remaining years of our lives.

2

It's bizarre how the death of a loved one can launch you into a period of introspection. Finding myself so angry with Tom for leaving me alone, thoughts of Uncle Izzy bubbled up, as if he were worthy of my time.

Uncle Izzy was my mother's brother who came for a visit one summer and never left. His long stay had something to do with a head injury he got at the mill. That's what they told me anyway – just one of the many lies, I'm sure.

He was the first bald man I ever knew. When he forgot to wear his hat, which was often, the scar was visible; an inch wide arc that extended over the top of his head, from one ear to the other, like the seam of a cracked egg.

Kids in the neighborhood called him 'Cueball' and would pester him for coinage when they heard the sound of the ice cream truck making its daily rounds.

As a teen-ager, I loved to dance and there were weekly dances held at our local high school on Friday nights. During the 60's we tried hard to keep up with the fashions worn in London. I once owned two fake fur mini-skirts, one leopard, and the other zebra, with black leather belts. A pair of brown leather pants, a pair of white go-go boots and several mini- skirts completed the collection.

One night I asked my Uncle for a ride to the dance and fifty cents to cover the admission. His selfishness stole a piece of my innocence, my first lesson about the reliance on others. I allowed his narcissism to wound a place in my heart that never fully healed.

He flailed about in such a fit of selfish anger, his top denture unhinged and fell to the floor with a thud. The sight was hilarious. I picked it up off the linoleum floor, blew off the dust and placed it in his hand.

He then forcefully threw two quarters in my direction, one of which rolled under the refrigerator. By this time he was red-faced, spittle hanging from a ten inch long red and white beard. Careful not to get too close, I reached down to fetch one quarter, now stuck up against the back wall.

Afraid he'd strike me, I decided to leave, as he again pitched another quarter into my face.

Refusing now to get into the car with this madman, I chose to hitchhike through the cold snowy night. So off I went in my white go-go boots and my fashionable zebra skirt, nearly freezing to death, until I was finally picked up by a cheerful Santa driving a VW bug. His name was Tom. We became friends, dated thereafter and later married.

Looking back, I concluded there are some families who should live together and some families who should not.

Perhaps my mother believed it was the right thing to do, or perhaps the family had run out of options. After all, she became her brother's keeper.

For most of us living during the 60's, hitchhiking was a way of life. Even if you had a car it most likely had a blown head gasket, sitting propped up on cinder blocks in your parents' driveway.

Not long after graduating from high school in Delaware, I set out for California to attend nursing school. I traveled most of the way by bus and would occasionally catch a ride with strangers when short on cash. I traveled light and fast to make it there by the fall semester.

Most people I met were kind, often taking me back to their homes where I could get some rest and a good hot meal.

Other times they weren't so kind.

Men thought I was easy, but after judging my stance, rethought their plans.

Women eyed my long hair and bell bottom jeans with either suspicion or awe, I wasn't sure which. My brown suede fringed jacket and shoulder bag didn't sit too well with folks living in parts of our country.

I carried my clothes inside a round suitcase covered with brick patterned contact paper that held the seams together. The one single strap snapped off outside of Oklahoma City. An owner of a hardware store gave me rope and helped me to fashion a harness for my suitcase, similar to a horse.

I arrived safely in California and completed my studies amid a social revolution that included parties, music, drugs, sex, rallies and protests. It sounds worse than it actually was.

But amid that chaos I found people caring for those who couldn't care for themselves, feeding and clothing runaway youth from all parts of the country and acquiring much needed medical care for the poor and disabled.

People worked hard to establish a new way of getting the job done with care and compassion; helping to make our country even stronger. I had found a new home.

Over the course of the next few weeks our plans started coming together. Mitch was the first to arrive and Gary shortly thereafter. Mitch's experience as a Paramedic was truly helpful and he added much needed emergency supplies to our medical stash, including a cardiac defibrillator he was trained to use.

Gary decided to keep his house in northern California and thought this might be a good get-a-way for us to escape the hot summer months in Arizona. Gary met with new doctors and started his treatment right away. Philip was in California wrapping up business. Doug and Sumana would arrive from New Hampshire a few weeks later, preferring to drive.

They had to coordinate their journey with the sale of their home and some antiques.

One thing was certain, that wherever there were elderly people, there'd be health problems. As chief medical resident of the house, I established weekly monitoring for measuring blood sugar, weight and blood pressure. This ritual proved to be very helpful.

We also agreed to make changes to our diets to lose weight and improve heart health. Having spent many years cooking at the fire department, Mitch was a great help and soon he and I did all the food shopping and out of habit, he happily cooked our dinner meal.

In addition to getting the house squared away, Carolyn acted as a tourist guide educating everyone about the area and helping to set up medical appointments. Thunder and Rocket were confused and barked themselves into a state of hoarseness, but they adjusted eventually. Carolyn took a particular liking to Thunder whom she began carrying in her jacket pocket all day long. Then one day she received a call from Philip in California. She relayed their conversation.

"Philip wants a bigger house. Thinking this house would be too small for all of us, he decided to buy the house next door – the one with the pool."

"It has four bedrooms on the ground floor and four bathrooms. With our approval he would draw up plans to adjoin both houses. There'd be an artist's studio for Sumana, a music room, a library, a spiritual place for solitude and a movie theatre. Philip would take care of the costs."

Carolyn was giddy with excitement, "We're going to have a pool!" We gave Philip the nod and set the plan in motion.

It turned out that Gary's cancer was not as advanced as he was led to believe. Although the radiation and chemotherapy recommended left him weak and readjusted his hairline, a full recovery was expected. We all took turns taking him to appointments, making his meals, helping him to bathe and dress and to do all sorts of daily activities.

With everyone's help, taking care of Gary was an effortless and seamless process.

While recuperating, Gary provided much needed legal guidance helping us to establish irrevocable trusts that contained durable powers of attorney, medical powers of attorney, advance directives and wills. He worked with Philip to obtain a variance and building permit as well as beneficiary deeds allowing property to transfer outside of probate in the event of a death, which in our case was inevitable.

Gary and Philip did some fancy financial planning that would allow each of us to stay in the house as long as possible. Just our monthly social security checks alone totaled over ten thousand dollars, more than enough to pay for food, utilities, house insurance and maintenance. Everyone brought their own personal wealth including pensions and in some cases, supplemental health benefits.

With Philip paying the costs for house renovations and furnishings, those funds far exceeded our living expenses. With two garages now, we had room to house four vehicles, more than enough for what we needed. Things were moving along nicely.

Still having unresolved questions about Tom's death, I decided to collect all of his medical records. Packages arrived for weeks, some with physician notes dating back to the early 1980's.

I spent time organizing notes, lab reports, test results and hospital discharge summaries in date order, so to create a visual rendering of Tom's health history and medical care for most of his life. I had doubts about this undertaking, but I had to find out more. There was so much about him I didn't know. What is it they say about Pandora's Box?

We soon learned that Philip's house plans would be just the beginning of the surprises that angled across our path.

One morning Thunder and Rocket announced the arrival of a delivery truck.

We opened the door to find a large trunk that had been shipped from England - no doubt Jackson's personal belongings. It took four of us to drag it into the garage. Carolyn, sitting on a nearby chair, reluctantly tugged at a large yellow envelope taped to the side.

Inside was a letter addressed to Carolyn from Francine, the mystery woman in England who had sent Jackson's ashes earlier.

The letter said that she was Jackson's fiancée at the time of his death, that they had lived together in England and that she would be coming to Arizona next month to meet Carolyn.

"Don't they have phones in England?" Carolyn asked sarcastically wondering why Francine never called to talk.

"She probably doesn't want to intrude on your privacy. You have to admit, this is an unusual situation," I said trying to curb Carolyn's frustration.

The silhouette of the trunk cast an ominous shadow and would not be opened on that day.

In reading Tom's medical records I learned for the first time that he had a congenital heart defect since birth. He would live a normal life, but knew it wouldn't be a long one.

No repairs could be made to correct the deformation and no medication could prolong its functioning. I wondered whether the defect was hereditary and if that is why we never had more children. We tried but couldn't get pregnant.

Perhaps this explains why Tom underwent a series of discreet sterility tests, all of which concluded he was incapable of fathering a child. He knew all along he wasn't John's birth father, but said nothing. He knew all along I had been unfaithful and after all these years, truth now be known, we were both guilty of deception.

Philip returned with new house plans, his luggage and a construction crew. He'd bunk with Gary and Mitch until the house was completed. We gathered around as Philip gave us the details, his voice excited, face flushed.

Most of the construction would take place in June and July, during which time we'd travel to northern California to stay at Gary's house where it was cooler. This would also coincide with a break in Gary's cancer treatment so we were free to leave.

Philip worked with Sumana, an artist with home decorating experience, to come up with a plan. The house would have a southwestern Mexican style décor with terra cotta floor tiles, dark wood furniture and trim with arched doorways. The doors would have black wrought iron hinges and locks. There'd be an electric fireplace, made of stucco, painted a creamy white, for those cool January nights.

Under Sumana's guidance we had carte blanche with unlimited funds to purchase new furnishings for the entire house. Doug would help with the construction and daily cleaning of the work site.

As I listened to Philip I couldn't help but think of the predicament that has befallen our lives, a situation I have yet to remedy. How would I go about telling him he was the father of a son he had never known? How would I go about telling everyone in this house that Philip was my son's father?

The whole task was too overwhelming, but it had to be done.

Philip will think I'm a liar and John will think I'm a slut. Everyone else will be distrustful saying, "Who is this woman we thought we knew so well?"

I would say nothing for now and wait to the very last before leaping off that cliff. I wasn't the sole accomplice in this caper. I was only human, and I couldn't begin to predict the outcome of an unfolding drama.

As the weeks grew into months, we all agreed it felt good to be living this way, with each person busy with their errands, yet knowing there'd be someone there when needed. This gave me a feeling of contentment and safety that I hadn't felt since long before Tom's death, as he spent so much time with patients at the hospital and I was often alone nights.

So many things I handled alone then: a sick kid, an intoxicated teen, eight years of practice and games for ice hockey, soccer and baseball, sitting on the benches eating meals out of a bag, consoling John during losses and applying first aid to his injuries.

Then there were the dog's seizures, squirrels in kitchen cabinets, encounters with skunks, porcupine, timber wolves and coyotes. The snow and ice storms brought power outages and the obscene phone calls sleepless nights. Many times I felt like a single parent and just tired of it all.

One afternoon I confided this to Sumana, who without warning, burst into tears herself. It appeared as though she too had something to confide.

"Doug was diagnosed with dementia. His memory problems advanced quicker than expected and now he appears to be having these long staring like episodes," Sumana said with tears flowing.

"I'm not so sure that working on the construction project is a good idea. I should probably tell Philip, but then Doug would be enraged."

"Would you tell Philip?" Sumana asked.

"Maybe we should tell him together," I replied. I made this suggestion more for myself than Sumana, since I didn't wish to have any long intimate discussions alone with Philip any time soon, being afraid of what I might say and where that would lead us.

Sumana had done a wonderful job organizing each of our personal belongings throughout the house resulting in a warm eclectic and comfortable style that made everyone feel like an Ivy Leaguer.

There was a large collection of music albums from the 50's & 60's, as well as big band era records our parents owned. Until the addition was finished, we designated a temporary area to music and set up a stereo system with headphones.

It also turned out we had a large collection of books and it took time to cull out those we didn't want. Most of the books we saved were older out of print books, most especially Mitch's collection of books on exploration of all points north, spanning from Greenland to Russia. Some were priceless first editions.

Gary collected books about the Civil War and WWII as well as books about nature conservancy and American history.

There were various large works of art, some of which Sumana painted that looked stunning on the walls and a few sculptures made of granite that Doug had shipped from New Hampshire to remind him of the granite state.

Other collectibles of antique furniture, mostly family heirlooms, consisting of cherry drop leaf tables and china cabinets, were tastefully placed around the house. Everyone was good about bringing only what they couldn't live without.

Consequently, we did end up with too many recliners, but were able to offer these in trade to a local store, replacing them with more suitable pieces.

We found that Arizona was good that way. Anything we could possibly want or need was within a ten mile radius of the house. Carolyn took a long look at how her house was changing.

"It's beautiful and I love it. All these things make the house look luxurious and I feel rich," Carolyn said while now carrying Thunder and Rocket in each pocket of her sweater.

"With these things and each of you here, I doubt that I'll ever feel alone again and that is all I could ask for," she added smiling.

It was sad for me to see Sumana upset over Doug. She was special in so many ways. Both of her parents were doctors who had practiced in New York City and she was an only child raised by a live in nanny. Her father was African American and her mother was born in India.

Adding to some of the social isolation she sometimes felt while growing up was the fact that she was movie star beautiful. Her physical appearance was stunning and her intellectual brilliance set her apart from others.

As a result Sumana was an outcast among teen girls or young women who resented her beauty, jealous she would steal their men. Ironically, she was pursued by men for just that reason.

These circumstances led to living a quiet sheltered life until she met Doug, who loved and respected her unconditionally.

Sumana and Doug moved in with us the first time in 1966 where she found an extension of that acceptance permitting her to expand her love and trust of others. This was followed by a flourish of creativity and the birth of her artistic talents.

I suspect, although I don't know for sure, that the estrangement from her parents was caused by marrying Doug; for the same reason she was now estranged from her own daughter.

Sumana had assumed a caretaker role in her relationship with Doug, a traditional role responsible for cooking, shopping, caring for their daughter and housekeeping. This would now change with our living situation, giving her more time to paint. Perhaps Sumana's career in social work was an extension of that caretaking role on a broader scale.

If I was granted just one wish, I'd give it gladly to this precious woman with the boundless energy and a great heart who has shared the gift of her benevolent spirit with others.

Someone once told me that at the end of your life the amount of friends you have could be seated around a table. My dining room table was ten feet long and the seats were vacant…until now. Another friend once told me that you know you're old when you start talking about bowel movements and medication.

So, we did this one night my friends and me, sitting around my ten foot long dining room table, talking about our surgeries and comparing scars, like ten year old boys at summer camp.

It was then we learned about Doug's experience that changed his life forever.

It all began one early February morning when Doug and Sumana went for a walk around the village green in their small New Hampshire town. The day was sun filled and trees were covered with snow and ice that clung to the branches. It was the quintessential setting, back dropped with rolling snow covered ridgelines, a robin's egg blue skyline and a Canadian chunk horse pulling an open sleigh.

They stopped to sit and Doug rested his head on the back of a bench to soak up the long overdue and much desired sunrays peering through the branches. Without warning a large patch of ice and snow fell from a branch above Doug's head, hitting him on the forehead and nose. The pain was excruciating.

Doug cried out, there was blood and Sumana thought for sure that his nose was broken so they went to the hospital to be sure. Doug was admitted when they discovered damage done to the bones in his occipital region.

While hospitalized Doug developed a rash all over his body like nothing the doctors had ever seen. They suspected it was a virus. The rash on his arms, legs and torso turned to a purplish crust and bubbled up like cheese on a pizza and causing him great pain.

Doug's journey was just beginning.

A paralysis took hold that prevented him from walking and using his arms. Eventually it worked its way into his lungs causing respiratory failure. He was placed on a ventilator to help him breathe.

There was not much for the medical team to do except allow the virus to run its course and manage any complications that would arise.

Several months into this medical misery he developed a high fever after contracting a bacterial staph infection. This prolonged any hope of recovery.

The paralysis climbed its way up to Doug's head, neck and ocular muscles and he remained hospitalized in a coma-like state for nearly a year.

All that time Sumana lived alone raising their pre-teen daughter named Gabrielle, as a single parent. The hospital was far from their home and free time became consumed with long drives, cafeteria food, meetings with doctors and visits to the medical library. Not much fun for a girl of any age.

At times Gabrielle rebelled, arguing with Sumana, refusing to visit her unresponsive father in the sterile hospital environment. She chose instead to be with her friends, pass love notes in class, wear heavy make-up and chase the teen-age boys who marveled at her beauty.

Sumana had no choice but to leave Gabrielle alone so she could be by her husband's side. She struggled with her loyalties to Doug and a duty to be a mother to her daughter.

Over time Sumana was absent at parent-teacher conferences and lost track of Gabrielle's attention seeking activities. Household chores diminished and eating out became routine. Sumana's responsibilities to her job and her husband took its toll on Gabrielle. Even when Sumana was at home her eyes held a vacant stare and she lacked the emotion and energy required to care for Gabrielle properly.

Sumana visited with Doug on week-ends when she could. But most of the time he was alone in his hospital bed with eyes shut unable to move while listening to the never ending pulse and whish of the ventilator pumping life into his lungs or an occasional alarm to warn of a change in his vital signs.

When the virus finally ran its course and the paralysis began to descend, his breathing returned allowing him to be transferred to a rehabilitation center where he stayed for one more year, to regain the use of his arms, legs and hands.

He had to learn how to walk and feed himself all over again. After twenty-one months, Doug finally went home.

But Gabrielle was lost forever.

Sumana described this time in their lives as 'maddening' and that if he ever got the virus again, "she'd pull the plug and put him out of his misery."

Residual pain remains in both of Doug's feet, but the virus never returned. He occasionally uses a walker when his gait is unsteady.

Doug also sustained a serious injury while cutting wood one winter in New Hampshire. When placing a chunk of wood onto the splitter to be cut, the piston came down too early crushing his arm and right hand. Had it not been for the excellent care given by air ambulance crew in route to the trauma center, he would've lost his right hand. Other than a decrease in sensation, a slight pinkish hue and a hand angled to the right, you'd never know the difference.

Mitch then told his dramatic story of the time his left foot was crushed under the rear wheels of a fire truck. This was a life changing experience in more ways than one.

The accident caused nerve damage and pain radiated up through his leg. He was taken off the ambulance and transferred to light duty, which eventually led to a permanent job as an instructor at the Fire Academy. Despite several surgeries and a year of physical therapy, the pain never stopped, resulting in addiction to pain medication. During this time, his marriage failed and his wife took custody of both sons, who were very young at the time.

Mitch overcame the addiction to pain medication, when some years later he had to have knee replacements due to arthritis.

Because of his propensity for addiction, he refused all medication, having to bear the pain without the use of drugs. It was then he started to drink in excess.

It was a long road, but Mitch has been substance free for the last fifteen years, except for the medical marijuana used for nerve pain. Without that, he would've taken his own life.

Mitch was never able to establish a relationship with his boys, who grew up without knowing their father.

But Mitch suffered from another experience that spurred his interest in collecting books about the cold north. His tale held us spellbound.

He had traveled up in the northwest portion of our country that included the icy straights north toward southeastern Alaska. A lot of these travels involved fishing for halibut, salmon or herring.

His buddy owned a fishing boat and in late August they set out for a week of fishing near Baranof Island. The forecast predicted clear skies, but this meant little to inhabitants of a region who could smell snow or rain before it is seen or felt.

At the end of the third day of fishing their catch was sold to the processor.

They tied up to a sheltered dock for the night adjacent to several long liners. After a night of boat hopping and partying hard into the early dawn hours, a deep sleep befell them all. The alcohol had deadened their senses.

The storm hit hard.

The winds reached gale force and the tide raced in throwing the boats from side to side as if they were riding a wild bull. The boat lines were taut and iron cleats were pulled clear out of the gunnels setting the boats free from the dock.

The instruments of their livelihood escaped from the cove and were rapidly being sucked out into the broad bay. Some men without thinking jumped into the cold water, swimming out to their boats. Others jumped into nearby skiffs and either rowed or motored their way. Those who boarded their boats coldly and stiffly were able to start the engines to join in the rodeo.

Believing they had a fighting chance, the Captains jogged their throttles while the crew bailed and set the outriggers – anything to battle the treacherous waves in any attempt whatsoever to save their boats.

Mitch put on a survivor suit and when it looked as if there was no let up, called in the SOS. He recalled that not long after he was tossed overboard and swam to a small island where slippery rocks jutted above the water and others below, razor sharp, tore holes in his survival suit and sliced up his legs.

A huge wave thrust him forward and upward into a large cedar tree where he remained cold and exhausted while overlooking the churning mix. At that point he had no way of knowing that his ordeal had just begun.

Mitch remained perched in the tree as pelting rain and snow poured down around him. Approaching the first stages of hypothermia, his body shivered and his teeth chattered to the point that physically moving became unthinkable. He could see a light grey horizon trying to break through but the sopping wet cedar branches blocked his view of the tumultuous sea.

An eternity later he recalled hearing voices – other men nearby in the surrounding bush. The men, who had been camping, approached from a ridge located from behind that angled up a steep hill. They had heard the call for help on their radio and walked down to the area, braving the risk of awakening a sleeping grizzly, to see if they could help.

Using rope they were able to hoist him out of the tree, dragging him to safety.

With the help of some matches and fire starter made from a soupy mixture of kerosene and sawdust, they were able to start a fire and prevent Mitch from dying of hypothermia.

His friend survived, but four others lost their lives and three fishing boats took their final voyage into the deep in that early morning squall. Despite the invitations, Mitch never went fishing again.

Being an environmental lawyer for most of his career, Gary was probably more at risk from a traumatic brain injury if a Supreme Court Reporter fell from the top shelf.

But, as it turned out, other than the prostate cancer, Gary only suffers from a crooked left eye that presented itself after a skydiving accident in the mid 70's, when parachute cords wrapped around his neck.

The women shared childbirth stories, the equivalent to shitting a watermelon. After adding the part about 'turning inside' out, the guys cringed and left the room.

While Mitch enjoyed cooking evening dinners, the task of cleaning the kitchen fell to me – a chore that brought me joy.

It was important for me to keep things clean and this became more challenging as our household grew. Things hadn't changed much - I had always been obsessed with cleaning, even when we lived at Peaceful.

This memory was made all the more clear one night when I ventured into the kitchen long after everyone had gone to bed. There it was, a ghost from the past, the empty glass of milk sitting in the sink. The culprit was still among us.

As in the other house, over four decades ago, there was always one empty glass of milk left in the sink at the end of the night. I could never find out who left it there, but I had a growing suspicion of who it might be.

Everyone had their little pet peeves. I recalled that Carolyn didn't like wet towels on the floor, Gary didn't like his butter put in the refrigerator and Philip was always putting coasters under glasses placed on tables.

Doug and Sumana didn't like cigarette smoke, but since none of us smoked this wouldn't be an issue.

I was a bit compulsive about having clean eating utensils, an empty dishwasher and a clean sink before going to bed.

Carolyn had a thing about the beds being made each morning and Mitch liked the newspaper intact. Every morning Gary tossed out the advertisements and Mitch retrieved them from the trash, until one day Mitch decided to have his own paper delivered. Unlike the old days, if a problem bubbled up now, we just threw money at it.

Philip was our technically savvy resident, making all of us wear emergency beacons as well as our own individual cell phones. We spent close to a full day setting up our phones, entering each person's information. While annoying, we were soon to find out how helpful these would be.

We also had other techno stuff like laptops, desk tops and one computer hooked up to a flat screen television.

The combination of my career as an emergency room nurse and my personality jaded me into believing, that at any given time, in any one person's life, a crisis was brewing. It may not happen tomorrow or the next day, but it was imminent. This belief was soon reinforced when the girls and I returned from a day trip.

We could smell the bread baking as soon as we pulled into the garage. Gary always baked bread on Sunday and the aroma, mixed with the smell of weed, was a familiar scent reminding us of a simpler time.

When we walked into the house the sounds of CCR were playing loudly on the stereo while Mitch, Philip and Gary were sitting in their chairs watching quail perched close to the window under the rose bushes.

Sumana went from room to room searching. "Where's Doug?" she asked impatiently.

"He was right here a few minutes ago," Mitch replied while turning down the music. It was then I realized we had forgotten to talk with Philip about Doug's recent diagnosis.

A few moments later, Sumana found Doug upstairs in their bedroom dancing ballroom style, naked as a jaybird, turning slowly in circles, with his arms outstretched, one circle after the other. He was enjoying himself, at peace in his world, with eyes focused on the ceiling.

Sumana explained to everyone for the first time that Doug had been diagnosed with dementia.

"Why didn't you tell us earlier?" Gary asked.

"I forgot."

"Well maybe he isn't the only one with memory problems," added Mitch.

Sumana brushed the comment aside.

"I knew about it and I forgot too," I added coming to Sumana's defense.

Doug wasn't being harmed in any way, but Mitch was concerned that the continued movements could lead to dehydration or exhaustion. Already we could see that Doug was sweating. We tried to sit him down for a drink of water, but Doug's dancing continued non-stop for two more hours. Mitch then helped us to take Doug outside where he draped wet towels over his head and shoulders and the dancing finally stopped.

Sumana said that he once danced in a theatre production where he did similar movements and wondered if that was important. We called his physician who agreed to come out to the house.

The physician explained that Doug required intravenous fluids and suggested he be admitted to the hospital for at least one night where he'd also undergo testing. He was taken to the hospital by ambulance.

We met Sumana at the hospital and waited with her through the night into the early morning when we found Doug awake and eating.

He didn't remember anything about the day before and all tests came back normal. He was discharged and given medication to thwart off future dancing episodes. We all went back to the house where we each took much needed naps.

Around three o'clock we began awakening from our naps, except for Doug, who was not in the house.

We searched the area surrounding both houses and checked with neighbors, but with no luck. Sumana reported that Doug's favorite jeans were on the bedroom floor along with his cell phone.

Wherever he was, he might not be wearing any clothes. With growing concern, we climbed into the cars and began searching the streets.

About six blocks down the road we saw the flashing lights of an emergency vehicle. Philip and I headed in that direction, while dialing everyone else to let them know. As we suspected, the excitement at the end of the road involved Doug, who by then was sitting in the back of a police cruiser, naked but safe.

Sumana cried when she saw Doug in handcuffs but we knew he wasn't under arrest. He was in protective custody for his own safety and would be taken to the emergency room.

A woman in the crowd told us her husband, now deceased, had done the same thing and warned us to be wary of combative behaviors.

She told us about an adult day care center nearby that was helpful to her and assured Sumana not to worry about his nakedness; that Doug didn't have anything they hadn't already seen before. This brought a smile to our faces. The Sheriffs were understanding and allowed Sumana to ride with Doug to the hospital.

We were told that Doug's episodes were seizure like, with only a short list of options available and doctors offered no assurances of when or if they would happen again. While Doug was not officially considered a weenie wagger, it was important to keep him safe while living in the community and that meant close supervision. They also reaffirmed the diagnosis for dementia without question.

We created a plan that was good for everyone. Doug would have one person with him every day and Philip installed alarms on the windows and doors that would emit a loud noise if breeched in the night.

Sumana called the local adult day care center, but discovered they had a waiting list eleven months long. Mitch agreed that on his designated day he would take Doug on long drives to places like Sedona or Yuma to see the mountain landscape and deserts or visit places like the cowboy museum or planetarium.

Physicians placed Doug on a pharmaceutical cocktail that would take a few weeks to reach full efficacy. They concluded that wherever Doug was during these episodes, it was a beautiful place, which helped to reduce our anxiety.

We weren't in the house twenty minutes when Doug began dancing, this time with his clothes on. We sat there and just stared wide eyed, still worn out from the day before.

Just when we thought we were beat, Gary stood up, moved the coffee table, and turned up the volume on some Motown. This forced us to get off the couch, raise our arms buoyantly, lift our eyes to the ceiling and rotate in circles.

We bumped into the windows, the walls and into each other, howling big "woo-hoo's" at the tops of our lungs. We held onto Carolyn, scooped up the dogs, threw away her walker and laughed until our faces hurt.

Sumana laughed loudly, the dogs barked and the quail gawked through the windows. But on this night, Doug did not dance alone.

3

Construction was beginning on both houses and Doug spent most of his days alongside Philip helping out with small tasks. After a few weeks Doug's medication took effect and there were no more episodes of naked ballroom dancing.

The more our house became active and full of life, the more skilled we became at living. Our lives were enriched more now than they had been for some time.

Gary was doing well in treatment and Carolyn was adapting to her grief. Her physical strength improved from swimming and allowed her to walk without a walker from time to time.

The time was fast approaching when we'd be leaving for Gary's house in northern California to allow Philip's crew to finish joining the houses.

Mitch and Doug spent many days traveling around Arizona, while Sumana spent time in Sedona and Tucson showing her artwork. Philip was busy with the house and Gary was wrapping up his legal practice.

Just when we thought our lives couldn't be more blessed, the dogs barked.

Carolyn and I didn't recognize the stunning dark haired woman standing at our door with silken hair that reached to the base of her spine. As she turned her body, we stared in silence, as a large pregnant belly, the size of a beach ball, emerged from her profile. It seemed as if we were seeing a pregnant woman for the very first time in our lives.

She extended her hand and chirped in a whispery voice, "My name is Francine. Would one of you be Carolyn?"

We stared stupidly at the woman who spoke in a coquettish British accent, eyes like a doe and legs like a giraffe, while caressing her bump, as if it were Aladdin's lamp. When Carolyn snapped out of her trance, she excitedly ushered Francine into the living room and made every effort to make her comfortable.

In typical British fashion, Francine cut right to the chase.

"The baby is due in a month, but as they say, it could be anytime. It's a boy," Francine stated. Carolyn just stared, unable to speak.

Francine continued. "Jackson and I were living together in England and were about to be married. She gently took Carolyn's hand and placed it on her stomach. "Say hello to your grandson."

Carolyn was gob smacked and all she could do was cry.

Francine acknowledged how overwhelming this was and apologized for showing up unannounced. Jackson was adamant about having his son born in America and they had planned to be married here, living for a few years in Arizona and then moving to southern California.

Francine explained further that Jackson had a large life insurance policy, that she and the baby were financially secure. Her plans were to buy a small house nearby after the baby was born, then work towards getting her license, as she was a registered nurse by training. She was tired from traveling and ready to settle down.

"You've come during the hottest weather of the year," Carolyn said wiping her wet eyes.

"I tried to come sooner, but had too much to do," replied Francine. "Did you receive Jackson's trunk?"

"Yes, I received it, but haven't had a chance to go through it. We're in the middle of construction. We've been busy." Carolyn added.

We discussed our plans for heading up north for the next two months while construction was completed.

"Do you have any friends or family in the area?" Carolyn inquired.

"No, it's just me and the baby. My parents live in New Zealand and have no plans on traveling right now. Jackson wanted to keep his family close to you – he talked about you all the time."

"Why didn't he write or call?" Carolyn inquired.

"Jackson was having difficulties at the University. There were threats to drop some of the classes he was teaching. His program was barely surviving."

The letter from Paris said he had a heart attack, but we'd never know for sure unless we read the autopsy report ourselves. I wondered if there was more to the story.

Carolyn spent the remainder of the day taking care of Francine, making her comfortable, fixing lunch and making certain she drank plenty of fluids. Francine shared a photo album and they spent hours looking at the life Jackson had in Europe. The years slowly melted away. Their attachment grew by the hour, and Carolyn learned the baby would be named after Jackson.

Leaving them to their privacy I walked over to the others who were spying on us from the kitchen. "Might want to start thinking about adding a room for a baby in those house plans," I suggested to Philip.

Francine returned the next day. Carolyn was interested in talking about getting the things they'd need for the approaching birth of baby Jackson. But on that day Francine was more interested in going through the trunk.

She pulled me aside to tell me that it was going to be emotional and asked if I could be there.

"Does this have to happen today?" I asked Francine.

"There are gifts inside from Jackson he wanted Carolyn to have," Francine replied with conviction in her voice. This was not to be a private moment.

We dragged the trunk into the living room and all of us gathered around, steeling ourselves, not knowing what to expect. When the seal cracked open, odor filled the room. The scent was familiar and we knew this would be a journey into the past.

Carolyn looked inside with a puzzled look on her face and then she reached in to pick up each item one by one. As if sent from the grave, the trunk contained stacks of Roger's letters sent to Carolyn from Vietnam bundled together in rubber bands; light blue envelopes outlined with red and blue stripes, stamped 'via air mail' across the front.

Roger's olive green jacket, affixed with his name tag and stripes in navy blue, still smelled of his cologne and made Carolyn nauseous. Unsure if she could continue, she reached down to find Roger's sketchbook of drawings, along with poems he had written and dried flowers inside.

There were glass beads, a book of her mother's recipes, headbands, leather bracelets and costume jewelry in a carved wooden box. There were music posters, Life Magazines, a long tie dyed rope belt Roger wore with his jeans, faded ticket stubs from a Janis Joplin concert and Carolyn's original red lava lamp.

The folded American flag that draped Roger's coffin was tucked into the far right side. The silence was palpable.

Water rolled down off her face as Carolyn reached down and took the flag up into both of her arms.

"I took the advice of a therapist who suggested I let go of my past. Before Jackson went to England I began that process, to move forward with my new life with Harold."

"These things had always been a reminder; like a death of a thousand cuts. I finally found the courage to toss it all one night. Jackson had the wisdom in his young age, to know the importance of it all. Like a thief in the night, he seized this collection, perhaps not yet ready to separate from his past."

"I should've considered his feelings too. In a way you could say I got rid of him too - sent him far away over the pond. My husband, my son and my past came back to me in boxes…I'm glad that Jackson had the chance to hold on to that time in our lives for a while longer."

"Did Jackson resent me?" Carolyn asked looking at Francine.

"Jackson never resented you, he loved you very much. I know he spent a lot of time reading the letters and poems Roger sent. They meant a great deal to him," Francine said with care and compassion. "It'd be nice if you could save them for your grandson," Francine added.

Carolyn finally exhaled and with a wide smile looked up at all of us, "We're going to have a baby," was all she could say in a softened bubbly voice, as if the weight of the world was lifted from her shoulders and total joy took hold.

F rancine handed Carolyn a gift from Jackson wrapped in gold paper with a large black velvet ribbon. He had planned to give this to her in person, but that day never came. It was a hard cover printed collection of the poems, letters and sketches Roger had sent to Carolyn. Inside was a handwritten inscription from Jackson: *"First there were two hearts and then me. It is all that I'll ever need; to know that I came from love and was loved."*

There wasn't a dry eye in the room.

Watching this scene unfold caused each of us to think about the deaths of our loved ones, how we had to let go of the past in order to move forward. It was the natural order of something we all must go through.

"So, what I don't understand is why you threw away the Janis Joplin stubs….in Chicago I think that's an arrestable offense," Mitch stated in typical form, adding levity to lift the mood on what was becoming an emotionally laden week.

"Look how small he was," Philip stated holding up Roger's army jacket. "We were all just kids."

Although Philip spoke very little about his tours in Vietnam, he did share with me that he had sleepless nights often thinking about Roger and his friends who didn't make it home. Gary thought about the guys who were able to avoid the draft altogether and the veterans, many disabled, who returned home to a country that had moved on without them.

Doug remembered when he received his draft notice and never understood why his number wasn't called up. Mitch's number was called up, but he failed the physical. When Roger was called up, he and Carolyn had just been married. It was a crazy time.

When someone you knew was being shipped 'in country', there was no guarantee you'd ever see them again…. except maybe on the evening news.

The afternoon made us think about simpler times, when our mothers baked fresh cake daily, lacquered with thick chocolate or vanilla icing and filled with strawberry preserves or grape jelly, lying in wait for us under the cake safe.

Gone are the times when dime stores sold only one kind of sneaker that came in only three colors.

We'd know it anywhere - the sound of the squeaky wooden floor that made us walk with an uneven stride pulling us left or right and the sound of voices echoing off faraway walls in the building that smelled like a damp box all year long.

Gone are the days when the most important decision of the morning was how to spend your only nickel on candy that lasted the longest. Gone are the days your mother shopped daily at the corner store, where the butcher cut the best choices of meat and vegetables were fresh.

4

I did speak with my son John from time to time keeping him abreast of my activities and plans for the future. Our conversations went something like this:

"How long are you going to stay in Arizona?"

"How long are you going to stay in Minnesota?"

"You know I'm still your durable power of attorney," implying that he could still have me committed against my will.

"You're not anymore. The people I live with are my proxies now."

"How many people are in the house?"

"Seven for now, but we may have two more. Carolyn's son, who died in Paris, had a fiancée named Francine and she's having a baby very soon. So that will make nine."

"Sounds like you're living in a soap opera."

"Oh, but there's more; Philip purchased the house next door and is attaching the houses together. We'll have more bedrooms and bathrooms, a library, music room and a movie theatre. We'll also have a pool."

"Are you still driving?"

"Not much of a need to right now. We have four SUV's and more than enough drivers."

"Have you had a chance to see an eye doctor?"

"We go to the doctor's all the time and everyone's bodily functions are doing just fine."

"How's your diet? Is it easy for you to get to the store?"

"Mitch and I do big food shopping weekly and we live just three miles from the food store and ten miles from any thing you'd ever need."

"Are you still smoking pot?"

"Oh yes. We all are. Carolyn has arthritis, Mitch and Philip don't sleep well, Doug has dementia with a slight nervous twitch and Gary has cancer, but he's doing much better now."

"Why do you get the prescription?"

"Oh I don't. I just smoke theirs. We have two miniature Chihuahuas named Thunder and Rocket and we're going to northern California for June and July to escape the summer heat. We leave at the end of May. "

"Where will you stay in California?"

"Gary has a house in the mountains - in wine country. It's huge with a large fireplace. I can't wait to visit the wineries."

"So, how can I reach you?"

"I'll have my cell. Did I give you the number already? I'll send you some pictures."

"So how long do you plan on living in that house?"

"Until I'm ten toes up Sweetie!"

"Maybe I'll come down for a visit," was the last thing he said.

I couldn't help notice that whenever John and I talked, he never mentioned his wife, much in the same way that Carolyn never talked about Harold. Now that Carolyn was having a grandchild, I wondered if I would ever have a grandchild. John and his wife's batteries were running low in their biological clocks.

The thought of Philip and I having a grandchild together was dizzying. Some days I just wanted to hide.

I dreaded John's arrival. What would the others say when they saw the color of John's hair, the shape of his face, the way his lofty shoulders and strong broad back held his head high? John's smile would be a dead give- away to all who knew that Philip once had those teeth.

Even though Philip had a scar that ran from the top of his forehead down to the left side of his face and under his chin, he still looked the same to us.

Philip was part of a unit that had come under fire in the night and was lucky to be alive. During an artillery barrage, while stationed in Pleiku, south of DaNang, Philip was injured when an ejected shell casing hit him in the head, peeling back the left side of his face and forehead, knocking out every tooth.

He returned stateside to recuperate from his injury, staying with his parent's in New York. His discharge date approached and despite the advice of the military and his parents, Philip re-upped and was returned to Vietnam for a second tour.

Philip was awarded a Purple Heart for his first tour and then later awarded the Bronze Star for valor when his unit cleared a landing zone for a medi-vac chopper while under gunfire.

Philip made all the flight plans for our trip to California. We'd take shuttles to and from the airports and rental cars would be delivered to us after reaching the house.

Now that Francine was in town, Carolyn thought it was best to stay in Arizona, but we encouraged her to bring Francine along, that she could deliver the baby up north in the local hospital. After all, she wasn't due for another month.

The day before we were scheduled to leave, Carolyn and Francine were shopping for baby clothes when Francine's water broke and they went to the hospital. Before we arrived, Francine gave birth to a healthy baby boy, all nine pounds of him. The chaos was electrifying.

Coalescing as a family now, we all shared in the immense joy at the birth of this grandchild. The whole matter just blew our minds. Francine would be coming home the next day, when we were scheduled to leave for California. Carolyn agreed to stay and all three would fly up the following week.

After leaving the hospital we spent the rest of the day shopping so that when Francine arrived at the house there was a decorated baby bassinette with all other baby paraphernalia and wrapped gifts inside one of the upstairs bedrooms. We talked about having Francine and baby move in with us at the house – even if it was just for a short while until she became oriented to her new life.

Everyone agreed to do whatever we could to bring Carolyn as much happiness as possible, to do what we could to make things easier. We loved her so much. There was nothing we could ever do or say to thank her enough for opening up her home, allowing all the renovations and giving us a home where we could live out our lives.

We were all feeling now that the older we got, the longer we wanted to live. Had we each suffered from such lonesomeness prior to this or did our desire to live flow from the wisdom of aging? Maybe it was the sunshine or proof positive of a plan going well. But, we *are* happy.

We arrived at Gary's house and realized we had more to learn about his life. His house was more than a mountain retreat. It was a mansion with an enormous amount of space for a single occupant.

It was very much like a lodge, decorated with dark wood interior and large windows on each exterior wall.

A porch sat beneath each window on the first floor and there was a large fireplace faced with river rock and fossils.

There were three living rooms and nothing austere about them. They were all tastefully decked out with fine leather furniture and antique tables, china cabinets and thick Persian rugs throughout. There were bookcases filled with books about nature, hiking, kayaking and mountain climbing.

In typical male fashion, there was a wooden canoe with a hole in the bottom hanging from the ceiling in one living room and a mountain bike with a flat tire hanging from another.

A chef's kitchen, the length of a bowling alley, was filled with industrial stainless steel appliances lining the walls on the south side of the house overlooking a lush green canyon. And even though Gary hadn't been there for quite some time, there wasn't one speck of dust to be found anywhere and the kitchen was stocked with fresh groceries. Growing more curious by the moment, I cornered Gary.

"So, tell me, did you hit the lottery or something? We never expected anything like this."

"You guys would find out sooner or later. I got lucky with some investments years ago and had a few inheritances. I was already doing well in my legal practice, so I guess it all worked out," Gary said as he retrieved food from the pantry.

He felt the need to explain further.

"I spent most of my working years living in the city. This house belonged to my parents. My mother grew up in upstate New York and designed the house to remind her of home. I've had a wonderful life."

"But I've also learned that you can't have everything. I have this immense wealth, but until you and the others came back into my life, it was meaningless. The cancer treatment gave me a new perspective," Gary said while wielding a fork in the air.

"Sometimes what you think you had in life isn't really what you had at all," I added as a wash of melancholy hit me. Beginning to feel weepy, I turned and left the room.

So, here it comes, I thought, the fall-out from the Philip drama. Gary followed me into the hallway and asked me to stop.

"Why so sad?" he asked. "Regrets about life with the doctor?"

"Oh, not really," I said avoiding the real issue. "He was never around, always jumping from one practice to another. The changes were hard, but overall we had a good life, I guess."

"Why did Tom change jobs so much?"

"I'm not really sure. We never talked about it," was all I could say.

Gary was such a stickler about details. In every household there is always one person who takes charge of making sure the car is registered and inspected, that the dog has its license and rabies shots and that driver's licenses or passports don't expire. Gary assumed that role in our newfound family.

Just before we left for California he urged everyone to update their passports. Doug never had a passport and Sumana's expired, but Gary wanted to make certain that if we decided to take a trip, we'd all be ready to rock and roll. It took us weeks to pull this together and I was glad we did.

My Minnesota operator's license was due to expire and a vision exam was required before I could transfer my license to Arizona. Perhaps the time had come. The thought of being totally dependent on someone for all my driving needs was crushing. I was concerned that my freedom and independence would vanish.

Gary announced that during our stay in California, we'd have a Chef and a server to meet all our food and beverage needs, along with a concierge and a housekeeper.

Outside where the wood was stored, there was a large ten person hot tub sunk down into the deck. In an adjacent room there was a massage table on the north side of the house overlooking one of the many rocky strewn tree lined canyons. There was a masseuse on call if needed.

We began most days with a wake and bake, our morning constitution, but on this day we took it out on the back deck in the afternoon. We sat with our feet dangling in the hot tub, our faces in the sun with a cool breeze at our back.

The server brought us each a glass of cabernet with hors d'oeuvres, announcing that dinner would be served at six.

"I feel like the poor kid in the neighborhood eating at the rich girl's house," I said while sipping my wine.

"I feel the same way," echoed Doug, who avoided his wine.

"That's because we are the poor kids and we don't feel deserving 'cause we're the ones that should be doing the serving," added Mitch.

"Not me," exclaimed Philip, "I pulled myself up by my bootstraps, provided jobs for a lot of people. I deserve everything that comes my way. Wait until Carolyn sees this place. She'll love it!"

His comment reminded me that Philip did have a difficult time growing up. His father often unemployed and both parents were alcoholics. Maybe that was why he was such a resourceful scavenger and very creative, it was a matter of survival.

As a teenager he was something of a gear head, driving used cars that were always breaking down and when other kids his age were out partying, he'd spend the week-end in the garage. Philip became his own man, served his country and worked hard to build a successful business.

Mitch carried with him at all times a fully loaded EMT bag we referred to as his make-up kit. He also brought along the defibrillator unit and mounted it to a wall. He was our own personal spring-loaded action hero, ready for anything at any time.

Of all the people whose career was such a contrast to their past, it was Mitch. As a young man he was absent minded, launching projects in fits and starts and never completing them.

While he did have a penchant for food and therefore cooking, he never could grow a garden and often had an unhealthy diet. He wasn't fastidious about his appearance or housecleaning, but was compulsive about hand washing and germs.

But the match between Mitch and his career was a miraculous one. He was caring, compassionate and skilled, quick thinking and swift. His contagious sense of humor helped to keep him and others around him happy.

Dinner was served and served well. The dining room was stately furnished and on the first night, we ate from antique gold rimmed china, replaced later at Mitch's request, for less pricey, less breakable and less toxic stoneware.

Gary announced that he had a surprise for me in appreciation for what I had done to support him during his cancer treatment. He presented me with two airfare tickets to British Columbia and two boarding passes for a small cruise ship that'll take him and me up the Inside Passage to Haines, Alaska at the end of June.

Everyone, including me, squealed with delight.

Gary said the ship was small, that it carried only fifteen passengers and because it was closer to the water, it would provide us with an intimate view of the wildlife and landscape. It was a dream come true.

The next morning Mitch got up early and went into the hot tub. Following that, he immediately took a hot shower. About fifteen minutes later he walked into the kitchen where we watched him fall to his knees while saying, "I don't feel so good."

His vitals were fine. We got him seated upright, placed cool towels on his body and gave him a cool drink. He came around slowly and we drove to an urgent care center right away. The doctors said it was most likely heat exhaustion, but during the examination they discovered a blockage to his heart that had to be removed promptly.

We were glad he didn't suffer a heart attack on our watch, as Mitch was the only one who could operate the defib unit. Mitch stayed in the hospital, had surgery the next morning and was home in about three days.

A short while later Carolyn, Francine, Jackson Jr., Thunder and Rocket arrived from Arizona with gear in tow. We spent our days close by taking care of Mitch and playing with the baby. Jackson was breast fed and rarely cried.

Mitch wished he could be breast fed, but instead had to adjust to an alternative diet, eliminating meat, adding tofu.

Francine reveled in being treated like the British princess she was, accustomed to all of it. Carolyn kept referring to the house as a 'castle' and wouldn't get out of the hot tub, adding that she was staying in California forever.

One morning she panicked when she couldn't find the dogs. It turned out the maid unknowingly scooped them up in a disheveled top sheet and sent them down the laundry shoot.

All we could hear was a faint muffled barking in the distance. Without her walker, Carolyn spun around, arms outstretched with her long hair swaying behind her repeating, "I can hear'em... but I can't see'em!"

We laughed until we cried. They were located later and both were safe and sound.

5

After spending two weeks shopping for clothing and rain gear, the day finally came in June when Gary and I boarded the boat in Vancouver and headed to Haines, Alaska.

We dressed warm for the not unusual impending wind and cold drizzle for this time of the year. We dined on fresh seafood and our drinks contained ice from nearby calving glaciers. We found a spec of dirt floating in my drink and were awestruck to think that it might have come from the days when cavemen walked the earth.

At low tide the mud flats stretched forty feet to the water's edge and when the tide rushed in, whirlpools would spin the water like a washing machine on either side of the boat. The days were bright and long and we watched as humpback whales fed on herring beneath bubbly water. Orca's flanked the boat, their great dorsal fins slicing the water.

Like having my own personal travel guide, Gary explained the history of the native tribes indigenous to the area and stories behind the exquisitely carved totem poles. He talked about deforestation, over fishing, global warming and melting of the surrounding glaciers.

We watched as fisherman in long liners and skiffs reeled in their catch while black bear and grizzlies walked along the rocky shores, digging for clams and clawing at salmon in the tributaries. The wind stole our breath as we watched   eagles nested high in the trees eye the terrain for food. They'd soar down to the water's edge where competition was fierce among the ravens, fighting for scraps of carrion, but would lose.

The gust from the northwest was unexpected, churning the waters along the passage as if the bottom had dropped out of the world. They were small at first, but the green swells grew larger by the minute. They continued to grow until the bow of the boat plunged into the tumultuous hollowed crater exposing the screws in the stern as water washed over the bow.

By order of the Captain, we were confined to our stateroom. Growing sicker by the minute, I was unable to stand or lift my head off the pillow. Eating was out of the question and the experience left me dehydrated and weak.

I began to think about Mitch's story and if we would end up perched in some cedar tree until morning.

The rain, now mixed with snow, quickly turned to ice before heading into the harbor. When we disembarked, I found that my legs were weak and my head dizzy, still swaying back and forth, as if I were still on the surface of the water. While the sightseeing was beautiful, there was no way I'd get back on that boat. The boat was stormed stayed for two more days and the hotels filled to capacity.

We chose to stay with a family who operated a bed & breakfast until Gary could arrange a flight by bush plane to Anchorage, where we'd catch a flight to Phoenix via Seattle.

The family members were decedents of the Tlingit tribe and told us stories about their ancestral history, their arrival on the coast and how they survived in the harsh living environment.

We were served meals fit for royalty and our hosts made us most comfortable inside their log home located on a hill overlooking water choked with bergie bits of ice.

This family and others we met during our brief stay were so kind, we honestly believed they'd give you the shirt off their backs if needed. Staying there was a joy for me in my sea sickened state.

I fully recovered only to learn that I'd be held hostage by the perpetual fog and torrential rains that kept me fermenting in rain gear, giving me a bad case of jock itch.

We headed north in a bush plane that seated four people including our luggage. It was a perfect opportunity to see the huge snowed covered mountains, black and pink granite crags and glaciers with their deep crevasses – the sight being what I'd describe as overwhelmingly beautiful, my face contorted in a fixed state of awe.

We were doing fine until hitting down drafts that plunged the plane, weighing not more than an Alaskan mosquito, downward some ten to twenty feet at times. The pilot reported this was not unusual and didn't seem worried, but I noticed a rabbit's foot and a St. Christopher's medal, dangling from a plastic Jesus on the dash.

Having seen Gary in a nauseous state in the recent past, I looked at him with growing concern. Sure enough, he barfed into the bags when the plane kept hitting the down drafts all the way to Anchorage.

The pilot reported that Mt. Redoubt volcano was about to erupt, giving a fair warning by spewing black soot and water from its lofty peak west of Cook Inlet. He added that we were flying at a good time, as flights were sometimes canceled when volcanic ash reaching as high as 65,000 feet, created a flying hazard.

We landed safely in Anchorage and decided to stay at a hotel until Gary recovered from being air sick.

Just as we were exiting the taxi, we felt our feet and legs moving sideways very slowly and creepily. The building above us swayed, first to the left, then right.

We were experiencing a great Alaskan earthquake.

Having lived in California for most of his life, Gary was more accustomed to earthquakes than I was. I had felt them before, but never like this. The quake and aftershocks registered a 5.1 and, other than childbirth, was the longest 30 seconds of my life.

Just about this same time, we learned that Mt. Redoubt finally did erupt and all flights out of Anchorage were canceled. Flights were leaving from Fairbanks, a full day's drive to the north, so we stayed in Anchorage for two days.

We spent our time visiting the Alaska Museum and planned to drive south to Seward, until we were told the volcanic ash was falling there. So, we spent the day at the Wildlife Refuge instead. Here we saw grizzlies, moose, wood buffalo, eagles, fox and caribou. They were doing great work at the refuge and Gary decided to make a sizable financial contribution to help them continue their efforts.

While heading back late in the day, we noticed people were just pulling into trailhead parking areas to start their hike or were fishing in a fast moving river nearby. The people were energized, as if just coming out of hibernation. It was pure 24 hour daylight now, the sun shining brighter and higher than in Arizona. To bear witness to this light of the sun was an opportunity of a lifetime I'll never forget.

We didn't get back to the hotel until 9pm, the sun continued to shine, the pace of the city quickened, bush planes were flying overhead and I got the sense that sleep wasn't part of the rhythm here, but that flexibility and strength was.

Despite the blackout shades, we hadn't slept well for days and as a result, were in such a stupor we couldn't drive to Fairbanks the next morning and missed our flight altogether.

We made arrangements to take a train north and stayed in Fairbanks for two days until we could catch another flight *somewhere* to the lower forty-eight – it didn't matter to us where, as long as we were headed south.

Most people dream of taking the train through Alaska, which traveled past Denali National Park, Dall sheep, moose, the little sleepy town of Talkeetna and the Chugach Mountain Range.

It would've all been so glorious had we not seen it from the back of our eyelids - even the weed didn't work.

The only flight we could get heading south to circumvent the volcano, was to Minnesota. We left Fairbanks at midnight thinking we'd get some sleep on the plane. But as we headed east, this was impossible because the beautiful bright sun was rising up over the clouds.

Just as our weary bodies landed in the twin city airport, it was time for breakfast and our sleep deprivation was turning into a medical condition. Our great Alaskan adventure had ended and all we wanted to do was sleep. Our next flight was scheduled the following morning, so we booked a room at a nearby hotel to regain ourselves and all we had was our carry on, as the luggage still lay under the sunny skies of Fairbanks.

Just when I thought that things couldn't get worse, I was surprised to see my son John standing alone in a line waiting to buy coffee. This just wasn't coincidental... it was supernatural.

"What a surprise seeing you here," I said as I sidled up to him with arms opened wide, approaching him for a hug. It was a short embrace, one of those hugs best left to greeting old acquaintances and colleagues you'd never wanted to see again. Obviously he felt the same way.

"What are you doing here? I thought you were in Alaska?" John asked while looking at Gary from head to toe. Gary extended his hand to John.

"Hi, I'm Gary, pleasure to meet you."

"It's a pleasure to meet you too," John replied while shaking Gary's hand. "So, why are you guys in Minnesota?" John asked quite sincerely.

"Gary and I are just finishing up our trip to Alaska. There was a volcano and we had to change our flight path, among other things. We're heading back in the morning," I said trying to size up his attitude before giving him any more information.

"How did your trip go?" John asked Gary with an authentic bright smile.

"Well, it was *the* great Alaskan adventure, complete with turbulence on the high seas and air, animals, volcanoes, earthquakes and even a ride in a bush plane," Gary replied while smiling too. "We met some wonderful people and ate great food," he concluded.

I turned to John and asked, "What are you doing here so early in the morning?"

"Well, should probably tell you now I guess. Sarah and I are getting a divorce. I just dropped her off, she's returning to Kentucky," John said while staring at the floor with both hands in his pockets looking despondent. "We're selling the house too," he added.

So, there it was, my hope for a grandchild dashed. What do you say to someone when you're happy they're getting divorced? Not knowing what to say, I then asked without thinking, "Did she take her cat with her?" John responded to my sarcasm with a wry smile.

He joined us for what turned out to be a great breakfast with us both engaging in congenial banter. He was actually quite pleasant for once and I wondered if he was taking a sedative.

As we parted John was curious when we'd see each other again. Although this chance meeting went well, I was growing more nervous by the minute as Gary talked with John; almost certain he could see the resemblance between John and Philip.

"We'll be in California until the first of August," I said.

"How about we make plans for you to visit then?"

Before heading off I managed to pull on my compassion pants.

"I'm sorry you have to go through the experience of losing someone you once loved. No matter what the circumstance, divorce is always difficult. Healing takes time, but it will happen."

He looked down at me and said quietly, "Thanks mom, but just so you know, I'm the one who asked her to leave." Just when I wondered how he'd fix his broken heart, my face lit up like an Alaskan spring morning.

After finally returning home, we spent days orienting with good food, good sleep and good friends to regain our strength.

6

Gary asked me to go for a walk one afternoon down to the canyon near a vineyard. He wasn't his cheery self and it didn't take long to get to the heart of the issue.

"Sharon, I have this vague memory in the back of my mind that you and Philip once dated back in the day. Am I just imagining this?" Gary asked sounding very much like the lawyer he was. "You don't need to tell me if you don't want to," he added.

"I don't mind at all. We had a thing going long before I married Tom," I replied looking down at the ground, not wanting to make eye contact. Knowing full well where the conversation was going, I decided to make the leap.

"We slept together the night Philip left." He didn't show me his surprise face.

"So, it wasn't over?" Gary asked.

"No, it was over. But Philip asked me to meet him that night down by the river, near the dock. He had received his draft notice and had a date to report for duty. He was certain he'd be sent to Vietnam and had thoughts about going to Canada. We were both very scared; the moon so bright I could see the color of blue eyes through his tears. We cried and then we made love," I said justifying our actions with a strength and conviction I hadn't felt before.

"That was the last time I saw him until he showed up at Jackson's funeral."

"Sharon, is it possible that John could be Philip's son?" Gary asked very solemnly.

"It's possible. I got pregnant that week. All these years, I never knew if he was dead or alive," I replied.

"I don't know what to do. If John shows up at the house, it'd just take a few minutes before everyone would know. He has Philip's smile," I added.

"The resemblance is just incredible. There can be no other explanation," Gary stated. "Let me think this through. Maybe I can come up with suggestions to help you come up with a plan."

"I just found out by reading Tom's medical records that say he was shooting blanks. He had kept his own secret."

"Sharon, have you been beating yourself up over this?" Gary asked.

"Yes, one, for having an affair and two, how could I not have known?"

"Sharon, you're not the first woman to ever have sex with a man before he went off to war. And you won't be the last. I suspect many babies are conceived before and during wartime and some of those children are likely to be raised by men they thought were their fathers. This doesn't mean that people were loose or irresponsible; it meant that they were loving and compassionate. After all, people are just human."

Gary was right. His voice was so calming and his words so comforting, I actually began to forgive myself. His warm gentle ways made me want to curl up onto his lap and let his arms envelop me. Was I falling for this little man with a crooked left eye with teeth as white as snow?

I finally forgave myself and accepted the way things have turned out, knowing that under the same circumstances, and given the same opportunity, I'd do it all again.

The next morning I awoke to find that my vision was blurry and attributed this to stress after my conversation with Gary, but the ophthalmologist told me this would be one of the first symptoms.

Before moving to Arizona a doctor told me I had a small non-cancerous tumor resting on my optic nerve. It's amazing the things that grow on you when you're having such a good time.

As it grew, symptoms would start to appear. In my case, the growth will need to be removed and when that happens there's a chance I could lose vision in at least one eye, possibly both. The plan was to wait as long as possible using medication to help thwart off symptoms.

During dinner one night, Doug entered the dining room and introduced himself to everyone:

"Hello, my name is Sam," he said while shaking everybody's hand as if meeting them for the first time. We looked at each other not knowing what to make of the situation.

"I'm now 'Rebecca'," Sumana added sarcastically. This new development was pushing her over the edge.

"The baby can call you Uncle Sam," Mitch chimed in. Everyone except Sumana laughed. When Sumana had the opportunity, she and I sat down for a much needed talk.

"For some reason Doug now calls me 'Rebecca'. He introduced me to some people we met at the winery and they became confused after I had just told them my name. It's becoming annoying," she added. "He's extremely pleasant in many respects, very polite and mannerly," Sumana continued, but it became clear that she was experiencing a great deal of anxiety.

We agreed there wasn't much to do except tolerate these behaviors and hope they'd be short lived. We talked about options and there weren't many. Sumana spoke with the California equivalent of an adult day care center, but there were no openings.

In the meantime, Philip took over the day trips with Doug to keep him occupied and safe, while Mitch was convalescing. We scheduled appointments for Doug with physicians upon return to Arizona, which was not too far off.

We decided to relax about the whole matter and allow Doug to be himself, whoever that might be at that moment. As long as he wasn't harming himself or running naked through the streets of San Francisco, we just needed to be patient and accept him the way he was.

Aside from Doug's odd utterances and occasional dancing, we had no complaints. He continued to be energetic and engaged in normal conversations about world events and the economy. Doug dressed well and kept up with his hygiene and ate all his meals. When he wasn't with Philip, Doug would browse the library and we'd later find him engrossed in a book in front of the fireplace. I'd seen stranger behavior from sleep deprived people in airports.

From what I know, Doug's family was Norwegian and while they had a strong work ethic, there was a great deal of poverty throughout his childhood.

Doug dropped out of high school at age sixteen to work at a grocery store. His mother died not long after and his father was injured in a construction accident, unable to work. When his father moved in with his older sister Doug finished high school and later attended a community college.

He was interested in working with people, so naturally was attracted to government service. It was a long road that led him to Sumana and from what I know, it was a match made in heaven.

As the days for our trip back to Arizona closed in, Sumana spent most of her time working with Philip arranging the final interior design of the new house. They spent long hours into the night talking and planning. I sensed that Sumana may have been getting much needed respite by distancing herself from Doug, getting the attention she needed from Philip.

When Philip wasn't with Doug, he was talking with the construction crew making certain all the final touches were done to perfection. Calls were placed to area merchants for delivery and installation of items we had purchased, artwork was to be delivered, appliances and window coverings were installed, with tiling and other floor covering to be laid. With the exception of final landscaping, the house would be completed before we arrived.

So while Philip and Sumana finalized our new digs, Carolyn, Francine and I spent time with the baby who was growing each day. As his features developed, Carolyn thought she could see her son's face emerge through the shape of the eyes and mouth, looking much like Jackson after he was born.

Mitch had decided to begin writing his memoir about his experience as a Paramedic in a large city and Doug stayed close to Gary.

My thoughts turned to the first time I met Philip, tall and as strong as an oak, with long legs and dark thick hair that hung to his shoulders.

He had steel blue eyes and like everyone in those days sported a full black beard with a mustache. His bear hugs so physically powerful, his heart would beat against your own.

Philip's energy was boundless, and even now he coordinated the house construction like a conductor leading an orchestra. He had a patient way about him and never once did he become angry with his crew on the project, as house building can often do to people.

$\mathbf{P}$hilip decided that the house in Arizona would be his last project. After that he would finalize his business affairs and settle with his insurance company for storm damage to his ocean front home in Malibu Beach, admitting the ocean had finally beaten him.

Year after year this tug of war resulted in so many repairs that it just seemed as though he were living in an unfinished house. More than once he replaced the stairway to the beach and three decks fronting the ocean. What was the point of living on the ocean if you couldn't access the beach or sit on your front deck?

When the sea tried to reclaim the west coast this last time, it had taken out the pilings and dislodged the steel beam that ran beneath the house. The roof trusses disconnected and Philip simply didn't have the inclination or energy to rebuild.

It was hard for me to think about this stalwart oak ever running out of steam and just when my thoughts drifted over to the 'what would have been' part of my brain, the dogs barked.

Early one morning a large box truck pulled into the driveway and Philip went out to greet the driver.

Philip asked each one of us not to go outside or look out the window, as the truck contained a surprise for the new house crafted by a local artist. Philip needed to inspect it before giving final approval for shipment to Arizona.

We were so curious we shouted out our guesses with hoots and hollers when all of a sudden coming up from behind us we heard an irritating whine. It came from Doug.

"It's a saaaan," Doug said standing behind us, today sounding like a cowboy, even though he was from New Hampshire.

"What's a saaan? Carolyn asked contorting her face.

"It's a saaan," Doug repeated. "If I told you what it was, it wouldn't be a surprise now would it?" he added sarcastically.

Our mouths were agape from the shock of Doug intentionally trying to ruin Philip's surprise.

"Don't say another word!" Sumana shouted as she held her hand up to Doug's face.

"Get me out of here before I kill him!" she yelped as she bolted for the kitchen. We had never seen Sumana so angry.

Gary quickly turned to Doug.

"Well hey fella' whadya' say we mosey on down to the car and go for a drive?" Gary said quickly. Getting him out of the house was a good idea.

"I'm not going anywhere," Doug responded appearing to be angry. "You 'all just want me outa here so Rebecca can spend more time with Philip," Cowboy Doug added.

The cowboy was jealous.

Just then Sumana came in from the next room shouting,

"I heard that you idiot and I'm Sumana, not Rebecca," she said pacing the room waving her hands in the air. Their barbs and jabs continued for a long fifteen minutes, at which time we called a time out and separated the two.

Doug admitted he was angry with Philip, jealous of all the time he was spending with his wife.

This was good to find out now as Sumana and Philip had planned on heading back to Arizona together a few days ahead of schedule to finalize the project. Doug, while in his current state, was still very perceptive. But in all fairness we too noticed that Philip and Sumana were spending a lot of time together.

We decided to divide and conquer. Mitch and Gary took Doug into one room and Carolyn and I took both Philip and Sumana to another room for a talk.

We managed to de-escalate the situation and it was agreed that Philip and Sumana would spend less time together and spend more time with Doug to ease his fears. We needed Doug to remain as calm as possible, to reduce the chances of him becoming disagreeable or combative. Doug apologized to Philip for spilling the beans.

Philip told us that no one, not even Sumana, knew what the surprise was, leaving us with a little more intrigue.

Sumana and Doug spent the remainder of the day together taking long walks and talking. By dinnertime, things were harmonious and nestled into each other shoulder to shoulder like two pieces of New Hampshire Precambrian granite.

We couldn't understand why Doug was talking like a cowboy and later started walking like a cowboy. He insisted that Sumana take him on several shopping trips and the impulsive buying streak was a new side to his personality.

He donned a large brimmed hat turned up on the sides with a fifteen inch brim surrounding an even higher crown. The hat came down over his ears making his head look childlike in size. He just flat out looked stupid.

But, being true to his nature, he didn't stop there. He searched far and wide until he found a pair of white snakeskin boots with pointy toes and three inch heels. This helped to create his new bowlegged gait, allowing him to dip his left hip and then his right, until he strutted hard heeled and noisily wherever he walked.

The leg tight denims accentuated his new look as did a ten inch brass belt buckle embossed with a horse and a lasso. His pants had only a three inch zipper so hung low on his hips. If it weren't for the tight legs, his pants would've fallen down around his ankles.

Sumana used an iron and a damp towel in an attempt to press the wings of the hat flat out straight, but it didn't work. Every time she tried to hide his belt buckle, he'd find it right off as if he had eyes in the back of his head.

We decided to accept this new cowboy into our lives and even though he didn't fit in – it didn't really matter. We just rolled our eyes and rolled with the punches. Yee Ha!

One night at dinner we talked about the news broadcasts and the housing shortages for aging boomers; our plans of taking care of each other looked upon now with fresh information.

Our living plan was no longer a matter of choice, but one of necessity, since there were no rooms available at the inn. We sought assurances about our future living plans now when the drama reached fever pitch and fear gripped our throats.

Sumana thought about Doug and how she couldn't find room at an adult day care. I thought quietly to myself about possibly going blind and Carolyn thought about how blessed she was that she didn't need to live alone.

We talked about our own personal situations and how our stories were similar to other families living in America. To provide comfort and alleviate our concerns, Philip gave up some details about our future home.

The house had a ramp in the front entryway and on a side entrance in case anyone in the future used a wheel chair. Hand rails lined the interior walls to assist people with mobility issues. Carolyn liked this idea. There was a security system installed that reset automatically every day at 7pm, reducing the chance of forgetting to arm the system. We'd still need to use our emergency gadgets in case of a fall or other crisis.

All of our bedrooms were on the ground floor. Should Francine decide to stay with us, her bedroom would be on the second floor. Each bathroom had a walk-in shower with a seat and could fill up like a bath tub.

There were pull cords next to the toilets in case of emergency, like those in a hospital. Each bedroom was large enough for two people and one hospital bed, if needed. The doors were extra wide for this reason. The kitchen cabinets and appliances were all waist level to avoid lifting arms or needing to climb onto a chair to reach up high.

There were telephones in every room and light switches at pillow level to avoid tripping over something in the dark.

The whole purpose for the house design was to provide a safe place for us to live, no matter what health issue would arise.

Mitch suggested that each room have a fire extinguisher and that a Knox Box be installed on the exterior of the house containing an entrance key for emergency personnel. Philip added that fire alarms and carbon monoxide detectors are wired into the house so batteries weren't necessary and suggested everyone be trained to use the extinguishers.

The silence that absorbed the room was a rare occurrence as we listened to Philip and Mitch run through the safety features of our future home, everything well thought out and in place, except for one thing that no one else knew.

My thought patterns over the last few days seemed to be embedded in a Shakespearian tragedy, which is why my personality was never suited for watching the evening news. Were we steeling ourselves for battle? Had the gauntlet been thrown?

Yes, in many ways, we were preparing to exchange blows with an unknown crisis that could befall us at any time and challenge our happiness, destroy our peace of mind, placing us at risk for whatever finality awaited us.

Good timing was never my style. Breaking my silence, with tears welling up, I then asked: "Do you think we'll have room for a blind dog?"

"Why would we want a blind dog?" Carolyn asked with her usual innocence.

"Do any of you have problems with your vision?" Philip asked.

Feeling like a student seeking permission to go to the bathroom, I lifted a finger and pointed it at myself.

"It's nothing too serious – just a non-cancerous tumor," I replied as Sumana and Carolyn gasped. I watched as they stared in my direction; their eyes filling with tears.

Gary and Mitch both placed their hands over their mouths as if it would stop either their emotions or their dentures from falling onto the table.

I then explained what to expect after surgery, not yet scheduled and how there'd be no effect on my driving, as that would end entirely.

"This explains why your son had been such a nudge," Carolyn stated.

"When will you need the surgery?" asked Philip.

"That'll depend on the new tests," I replied. "So, what if I need a blind dog?"

"That shouldn't be a problem as long as the dog isn't blind," Mitch stated sarcastically.

"We'll get the best trained dog that money can buy, and by the way, they're called service dogs," Gary quipped while touching my hand.

"The house will be easy to navigate for someone with vision problems. With a dog, it'll be a piece of cake, as long as there are no rugs placed on the tiled floors," added Philip.

Listening to Philip helped remove my brain from the doomsday gutter and allowed me to see, in all its beauty, our house of the future. It was a good plan and we'll make it work.

Just knowing I didn't have to endure this alone felt as if the weight of the world was lifted from my shoulders. Just knowing I could live here with my friends, if I lost my vision, bestowed me with a comfort and peacefulness that a child must feel when held by its mother.

After dinner Gary came over and expressed his sorrow adding that he felt bad I had missed the opportunity to see Denali on the trip north. He asked me if I wanted to return before my surgery. I declined that offer, but Gary already had plans on going to Banff, Alberta in Canada and wanted to take me along.

He assured me - no cruises, no bush planes and probably no earthquakes. We'd fly into Calgary, drive a few miles west and enter the Banff National Park.

We'd stay at a popular hotel along the shore of Lake Louise, a blue-green glacier fed lake surrounded by towering ridgelines, with a glacier overlooking the end and bordered by hiking paths.

Gary was becoming my new found traveling partner and lifted my spirits. There was only one catch: Philip would need to know about John before we left.

Gary suggested I release this burden once and for all, allowing me to enjoy the trip and have some peace of mind before the surgery; to help promote a full recovery and prepare for the lasting effects of possible vision loss. Banff, Alberta was the place to do this, a place of enchantment, a heaven on earth. He assured me that our visional pursuit would be permanently lodged in my memory, providing a lasting remembrance of unsurpassed beauty to last a lifetime.

My thoughts turned to events of the days ahead, scheduling an appointment with the ophthalmologist, packing for Arizona, planning for Banff and setting the stage to rock Philip's world forever.

Here in California would be best, so as not to tarnish his swan song gift created for all of us. Philip was scheduled to leave for Arizona the next day. I'd tell him on this moon lit night, while looking into those steel blue eyes that captivated me so long ago. I wondered in silence if Philip could feel the tsunami coming his way.

As evening approached everyone went to their own separate corners of the house doing whatever it was that brought them comfort at the end of their day. I found Philip sitting on the back deck alone, scotch in hand, relaxed and taking in the scenery disappearing under a setting sun.

"Let's go for a walk. I have something I need to talk with you about," I said.

"Is this about the blind dog?" he replied.

"No. This has to do with you and me," I said straight on, looking him in the eye.

There was silence as we left the deck and headed toward the front of the house and down a hillside covered with pebbles and tufts of green grass.

When we cleared the house I turned back and saw Gary and Carolyn's faces peering through a second story window, reminding me there is no privacy when you have a large family.

Philip and I found a small deck and seated facing each other in two wooden chairs.

"Do you remember our last night at Peaceful, before you left?" I asked.

"Yes, I remember as if it were yesterday," Philip replied.

"We lost touch after that, remember?" I said setting the stage.

"Yes, of course I remember," Philip said putting down his glass.

"I got pregnant with John that week." There, I had said it.

"So, what does that have to do with me?" Philip asked.

"You really can't be that dense," I said holding both of his hands in mine.

"Are you saying that I'm John's father?" Philip asked.

"Yes. But I didn't know until I saw you. John and you could be twins. There's no denying it," I added handing him photos of John.

"You can't be serious," was all he could say.

I explained Tom's medical records, the sterility tests and his heart condition, how we tried to have another child, but couldn't. Philip wondered if Tom had a vasectomy without my knowing, not wanting to pass along a potential hereditary heart condition to a child. In my current state, I believed that anything was possible.

"How long have you been worrying about this?" Philip asked as he put his arm around me.

"Since I first saw you enter the doorway at the funeral," I said starting to cry. "Carolyn and Gary also noticed," I added. "They encouraged me to tell you."

"Have you told John?" Philip asked.

"No. Not yet. Gary thought I should tell you first and let you decide," I responded.

"He's a good man. Good advice," Philip said about Gary.

"I haven't told anyone else. Maybe that's something you should also decide," I added.

"I wonder if John and I should get blood tests or something. Whadya think?" asked Philip.

"I honestly don't know. That would mean we'd need to tell John," I replied.

"So why don't you tell me a little bit more about this son of mine?"

"Well, he was a great kid, healthy, an athlete in high school, played all the usual sports with ice hockey being his favorite - still a big hockey fan living in Minnesota. He is getting a divorce, his wife was from Kentucky. He does well financially working in government, but I don't think he's really happy. He received his Master's from Northwestern. I think he resented Tom for spending too much energy at work, having less time for all of John's sports," I said.

"Well, what did he study in college?" Philip asked. "Medicine? Like Tom?"

It was at that moment I saw for the first time that Philip and John had the same hands.

"By training, he's an architect, just like you," I said when the tears started flowing.

We stood up and Philip put both arms around my shoulders holding me tight.

"It'll be alright," he said with calm and compassion in his voice. "So, does this mean we are officially dating?" he added jokingly.

"No. Maybe in our next life. Besides, I think I have a crush on Gary," I replied.

"The way I figure it, you can be my baby daddy and Gary can be my sugar daddy," I added now laughing.

Philip agreed to tell everyone in the morning about his newfound status and would think about a strategy in the coming days on how to approach John about this delicate, life changing matter.

Morning arrived and we started the day with a candle lit champagne breakfast using the fine china, all in celebration of Philip's hard work giving us a new home. Each of us gave Philip a handwritten note expressing our gratitude for all he had done, a good send off before his flight to Arizona.

There were nine of us around the table, including baby Jackson. Carolyn was excited, Sumana was quiet and Francine looked radiant. Doug was on an even keel and Mitch was his usual jovial self.

Gary wore a contented smile, seeming to be at peace with the world. The cancer treatment had stolen his bushy silver locks and eyebrows, but no man could've been more aristocratic in appearance. His skin tanned a golden hue, his lean small frame sporting tasteful attire that never crumpled, like a mannequin in a store window.

Philip stood to make his announcement.

"By this time next week we'll be together in Arizona for new beginnings, in a new house that for some may be our last. A house is just a house. What's important here is our commitment to each other and the way we have chosen to live out the remaining years of our lives. We have two choices: we can either make it a hassle or make it great. I choose to make it great," Philip said as he lifted his glass to a toast. We all raised our glasses in agreement.

"Now I have something else to tell you, that I just learned myself last night," he added. "It turns out that I'm the father of Sharon's son John. It's not all that complicated.

"We had sex the night I left Peaceful. We haven't told John yet."

Sumana's eyes opened wide.

Gary and Carolyn nodded their heads in agreement with Philip's style and approach and others stared straightaway, remaining silent.

Just when I thought it was best for some things to remain silent, Doug, in his usual filterless annoying voice asked,

"Well, I guess ya'all'll be gettin' married then?"

Sumana cringed and placed the full palm of her right hand up to within an inch of Doug's face, a signal for him to stop talking. Philip wasted no time walking stiffly to the other side of the table stomping his boots loudly.

By asking that one question, Doug had taken a perfectly innocent situation and tried to make it appear distasteful, as if by not getting married, we refused to take responsibility for our actions that night. Morality holds us all hostages, regardless of our age.

Placing his face close, Doug could feel Philip's hot breathe in his ear.

"I asked her to marry me, but her heart belongs to someone else," Philip embellished while offering a glance over in Gary's direction. "Let's not make it a hassle Doug."

This was not the first time Doug had angered Philip, and for an instant I thought Philip was going to punch him.

Doug swallowed hard and said nothing for the remainder of the day. Philip left for Arizona that afternoon, while Sumana stayed behind.

In the days that followed we began packing for the trip home. We had a farewell dinner the night before to celebrate our new beginnings. Later, while sitting in the hot tub, Sumana sat down next to me with a concerned look on her face.

"I have a tremor in both of my hands," she stated holding her hands out for me to see. "It started about two weeks ago, first the right, then the left, now both at once," she added.

"I wonder if it could be stress," I said, trying to downplay her fears. I could see that both of her hands were definitely shaking tremor like. "Has it had an effect on your painting?"

"Yes. I switched from oils and acrylics to water color. Believe it or not, the tremors help with the blending," Sumana said smiling while still looking at her hands.

"We'll have to get you an appointment with a neurologist when we get home," I stated.

"I'm sorry for what Doug said the other day at breakfast," Sumana said.

"You don't need to apologize for his actions. We just have to remember that he's not himself these days. What's he doing now?" I asked.

"Sitting in the rocker, listening to music," she added.

7

While sitting on the plane I noticed that Sumana first held her hands together, and then she'd sit on them for a short while, and then later wrap her arms around herself to keep her hands from moving. She seemed a little more anxious than usual.

Without a filter, there was no predicting what Doug would say and without a muzzle, there'd be no way to prevent it. Trapped in an airplane at 35,000 feet presented new challenges.

"Can't you' all keep those kids quiet?" Doug said loudly to a mother of two.

"Is that all we get are peanuts? I want some real food," Doug said loudly to the attendant.

"Look at those tattoos. I bet she has a tramp stamp," Doug stated harshly in the direction of another woman.

Sumana had a great look of anguish upon her face, the look that comes from being responsible for another person who exhibits unexplained behaviors or utterances in a public place. This went on for a few minutes until Sumana saw that Doug was inhaling more air, and quickly placed her trembling hand up to his face. Doug reached up to push it away.

"Put yer hand down...I didn't say anythin'....You' all can't stop me from talkin' all the taaam," Doug said to Sumana. "I'll say what I want."

I was sitting in the aisle ahead of them to the right and I could see as Sumana's eyes welled up. She stiffened in her seat; head faced forward staring at the seat in front of her. I wondered if she was reaching her breaking point.

Feeling the need to intervene I spoke with the attendant who allowed us to exchange seats so I could provide much needed respite.

Doug sat without talking, but began to fidget instead.

It occurred to me that perhaps he was becoming more agitated by the flight and afraid he'd leave his seat, I asked the attendant to activate the lap belt 'on' sign, because without that, Doug refused to comply. She understood and complied with my request.

With Doug now belted in, calming him down was my goal. I gave him another dose of his medication and surrendered my headphones so he could listen to music. While holding his hand, he began to rest peacefully and eventually was lulled into a deep sleep.

Just when I began to relax myself, he began snoring loud enough to disturb everyone on the plane who stared in our direction. How it happened, I wouldn't know, but he snored with an annoying twang.

Philip made arrangements for a shuttle to pick us up at the airport and greeted us on the sidewalk. We barely recognized the house.

There was a grand pillared entrance with double doors opening into a large foyer. There was a round granite table from New Hampshire adorned with silk flowers.

Something large hung on the wall under a sheet and the house smelled of fresh paint, stucco and new tiling.

"It's a mansion," Carolyn shouted, her voice echoing down the hallway.

"Whoa," was all that Mitch could say while his head spun around in all directions.

"Very nice," Gary added.

Philip stood at the end of the foyer holding a tray of glasses filled with champagne. On another table lay trays of fresh fruit, chocolate covered mangos, chips, salsa and a spinach quiche. He poised himself in front of the draped sheet on the wall to make an announcement.

"Oh, here we go agin'…anotha' speech…," Doug chirped. Sumana gave him the evil eye.

"First there was Peaceful. Now I give to all of you, 'The Wrinkle Ranch', Philip said as he raised his glass and pulled the sheet away revealing the sign that caused such a stir.

We were spellbound.

All of us, even Doug, let go with screams of laughter, when all of a sudden, Carolyn yelped,

"Where's the bathroom, I'm gonna' pee my pants," she said while hobbling down the hallway, her laughter bouncing off the walls.

The sign was stunningly beautiful, a stained white cedar carving with raised letters, trimmed in dark brown with gold highlights.

Gary put his arm around me and spoke quietly into my ear. "So is this where it all ends?"

"It beats chair exercises and bingo," I said.

"Did I ever tell you that bingo made me horny?"

"That doesn't scare me as much as how you discovered that."

Mitch looked over and said, "Philip, you're one classy guy and Sumana, you have done a wonderful job decorating this place." We all raised our glasses to Sumana.

"Very well done," Gary repeated over and over.

"Not bad for an old coot," I added motioning to Philip.

"There's more," Philip and Sumana said at the same time motioning us toward the hallway.

The hallways and living room were lined with large framed photographs and bits of memorabilia.

84

On closer inspection, we saw Carolyn and Roger's wedding day, Carolyn and Jackson, aged one year, Christmas 1969 with all of us sitting around the tree, Mitch and me on the front porch at Peaceful shucking corn, Doug, Sumana and Philip sitting on the dock, Carolyn and me with our heads wrapped in scarves sitting in the row boat dubbed the "USS JFK", holding up a coconut.

There was a picture of Tom on the beach with his fishing pole, bushy hair and a deep tan and another photo of us sitting on the front porch on a hot summer day.

There were framed posters of famous musicians, a peace sign embroidered into a tie dyed fabric and framed movie posters featuring the Hollywood stars of our time. There was a banner that read, 'Make Love Not War'.

Another frame held a collage made of newspaper clippings: Jack, Bobby and Martin Luther King, Kent State, the first orbit of the earth and moon landing, the march on Washington, the fight for civil rights, the Civil Rights Act of 1964, photos of burning flags and bras, Woodstock, Vietnam and Chicago '68. We shuffled around the rooms in total amazement, each of us thinking back to another time so long ago.

"Is he gonna' make anotha' speech?" Doug said as Philip gathered us all around. Sumana told Doug to shut up.

"I'd like to think that 'The Wrinkle Ranch' is a museum to us all…our legacy and when we're gone, others can take our place," Philip stated with teary eyes and a flush face.

At the end of a hallway, next to a window, there was a large framed print that contained a written black script on white poster board.

It was a poem that Roger wrote to us before he left for Vietnam. His poem captured the essence of our life at Peaceful and our love for each other:

Constant Thoughts

When I end another day alone,
I'll think of the things I did with you,
It's funny how it brings tears to my eyes,
But never did at the time.
Each day we live, each thing we do,
Is just more to be considered the past,
Every minute that passes,
Becomes a memory...
If something is done worth remembering.
Life is a puzzle,
But what do we do?
....We just keep trying to put the pieces together,
While time is passing by,
And we get older.
Was that my childhood that passed by yesterday?
Or was it my constant thoughts of tomorrow?
Will fate have in store for me,
the same as for you?
For we all had good times together,
My constant thoughts are your constant thoughts.

Philip added one other special item that caught our attention.
"Does anyone know what a tontine is?" he asked.
"I know the legal definition," Gary replied.
"Well, a tontine can also be something that is left for the last man standing – in our case...the lone survivor."
"This is very depressing," I added.
"We're going to live forever," Carolyn whispered in my ear.

"I had something specially made for the last person surviving in this group…a gift they will open alone," said Philip. "You all need to make me a promise."

"Like a time capsule?" asked Carolyn.

"No. It is a gift to all of us," added Philip.

"From who?" asked Carolyn.

"I guess it's from Philip since it was his idea," I said.

"It is specially wrapped in a leather casing that cannot be opened until that last man is standing," Philip concluded.

"We don't have to actually be standing, right? We can be seated in a wheel chair," stated Gary winking to the others.

"You have to promise me you won't touch it until then. It arrives tomorrow and I will place it on the top shelf in the solitude room."

We all agreed the tontine would be opened by the sole survivor.

We spent the rest of that day orienting ourselves, unpacking and trying out the comforts of our new furniture.

Carolyn framed the ticket stubs from the Janis Joplin concert and hung them in our hippie hall of fame and then headed straight for the pool with Thunder and Rocket resting comfortably inside the pockets of her sweater.

Francine settled in upstairs to stay with us for the time being and the guys settled in to their own individual rooms.

Creation of the Wrinkle Ranch was a remarkable achievement filled with heartfelt memories.

How lucky we were to be here together, living in a house such as this. I could hardly wait to see what the next day would bring.

One week later Gary and I arrived in Calgary and within fifteen minutes of driving past the entrance into Banff National Park, a cinnamon colored grizzly bear, weighing maybe 250, walked briskly in front of our car. Before I inhaled to take a breath, it was gone.

The two lane roadway was flanked by large elk making bugling sounds and big horned sheep sitting regal like. A young fawn, born that spring still wearing white spots on its back, trailed behind our car blatting, his hooves tapping hard on the blacktop.

We saw ravens and magpies foraging for food and antlered deer crossing frequently. I had to remind myself that this wasn't a zoo – this was the real deal, an actual forest without a fence.

In reviewing information about the park, I learned about the dangers of mountain lions and how hikers had to take special precautions to protect themselves, making themselves appear larger, by raising their hands or standing on a large rock.

There were suggestions about whether or not to wear bells on your day pack or carry bear spray. When I explained all of this to Gary, he didn't seem the least bit concerned.

"Have you read this information about grizzly bears and mountain lions?" I asked.

"I don't need to worry. All I need to do… is run faster than you," he replied.

We started our mornings checking the local bear report warning hikers to avoid areas where grizzlies were foraging that day.

During this time of the year, it was berry season, time for the bears to gain their winter stores before hibernation. We decided not to do any major hiking trips deep into the forest, but instead took short walks along the path next to Lake Louise and back behind Bow Lake.

Even then we put rocks in a can, shaking it occasionally to make our presence known.

Another tourist volunteered to take us for a paddle in a canoe out onto Lake Louise. The water looked like jade green colored milk and we could hear loud booms made from ice calving from the glacier at the end of the lake.

The beauty of the surrounding mountains was different than the mountains in Alaska. Here, they were much closer, as if you could reach out and touch them.

Another lake surrounded by mountains called 'The Valley of Ten Peaks' towered over Moraine Lake, the most stunning vista yet.

We took the ski lifts up to a mountain top and were able to see the expanse of the Canadian Rockies. Just when I thought the views couldn't be more beautiful, we took a day trip up the Icefields Parkway to Jasper National Park.

Gary was right in that this was a place of enchantment. The beauty was remarkable. The parkway is a two lane winding highway that traverses through mighty high ridgelines, some of which launch dangerous avalanches onto the road in winter and spring. The mountains were snow capped with threading glaciers reaching into the lakes below.

Along the parkway we watched a small black bear, nose to the ground, either searching for food or tracking a scent. We took a tour bus and were able to get out and walk onto a gigantic glacier. We bent down on our knees and placed our ears next to the ice beneath us and heard rumbling noises and then loud cracking sounds, like sap filled wood snapping in a bonfire.

We ended our days with dinner at the hotel, overlooking Lake Louise. This place was quickly becoming my favorite.

We went shopping in Banff where I learned for the first time you could buy a sweater made from the hair of muskoxen, called qiviut.

One day we had a picnic and sat along the banks of the fast moving blue waters of the Bow River. Another day we ventured into British Columbia and had lunch high up on a mountain, getting there by ski lift.

We didn't take many photographs, choosing instead to buy large picture books produced by local photographers who were able to venture into areas that were out of our reach.

"Why should we buy these books when I may lose my ability to see them?" I asked.

"Let's get them just in case," he added.

We finished up our trip dining in an historic hotel, browsing book shops, visiting museums and visiting other nearby parks. The entire trip was more than I could've ever imagined and the beauty was astounding. Doing my best to avoid melancholy, we headed back to Arizona to settle down for a few weeks, or so I thought.

"Sharon, would you consider traveling east to get a second opinion or to have the surgery? My mother had eye surgery and had great luck with a specialist in Boston. Would you consider it?" Gary asked. "We'd go together."

For some reason, Gary always knew what was best for me.

When we got back to the ranch, everyone was settled in. Mornings were spent having coffee and breakfast poolside, under the palm trees, as Carolyn did her daily walking and strengthening exercises in the pool.

For safety reasons we all made a pact to never enter the pool without help or swim in the pool alone without someone nearby to watch.

Mitch gladly assumed the role of lifeguard for Carolyn each morning and also helped her and the dogs climb up onto a raft to soak up the sun.

Each of us assumed a responsibility for the house. Since Gary paid the bills, he was in charge of delivering our mail.

Mitch still cooked dinner and he and I were still doing the food shopping. Carolyn, Doug and Sumana worked on the landscaping and gardens. Philip took care of the cars.

I continued to clean the kitchen at the end of the day. Francine was a bit compulsive, bordering on addiction, when it came to doing laundry, so we embraced her energy for this task.

We did find it necessary to hire a cleaning crew to come in every Saturday morning, as we were unable to do all of the floors and bathrooms. Because each of us moved at a different pace, albeit a slow one, answering the door was always a crap shoot.

One day, the dogs barked and Philip, Doug, Sumana and I went to the front door at once. Philip got there first and when he opened the front door, we saw with great horror, my son John standing there. We were speechless, with nowhere to run.

"Hi, I'm John," he said with a large smile across his face. Philip turned to me again, wide eyed and then turned back to look at John, as if he saw his own reflection in a looking glass. We both wondered what to do next…when fate intervened. It was then I learned about the fine line between love and hate.

"So, you're Sharon's son," Doug said. "That means that Philip's your daddy."

"No, my father passed away," John said, looking puzzled.

Philip then got between them and attempted to pull Doug out of the foyer and back into the house, when all hell broke loose.

"That may be so, but Philip was the stud," Doug yelled loudly. "Let me be the first to introduce you to your daddy," he hurled in a loud voice.

Doug never knew what hit him.

It was Sumana who struck the first blow, cuffing Doug in back of the head with an open right palm, knocking his eyeglasses to the floor. Within seconds Doug and Sumana were rolling on the floor on top of each other, Sumana was screaming and punching Doug's arms and chest, Doug yelling at Sumana to stop.

"Sumana stop hitting me, Sumana stop it," Doug repeated over and over. Then she suddenly stopped thrashing and stood up.

"You called me Sumana!" she cried out to Doug. We also noticed that Doug wasn't talking like a cowboy.

She had literally knocked it out of him.

Gary entered the room after hearing all the raucous. He acknowledged John and invited him inside. "What's going on?" he asked John in his lawyer voice.

"The guy on the floor said that Philip was my father and that beautiful woman hit him in the head," John said studiously while pointing to Doug and Sumana.

Gary added a touch of decorum to the matter, taking John into the quiet solitude room and walking Doug and Sumana to their bedroom. Gary then walked Philip and me to the solitude room and suggested we sit down in private with John to offer an explanation. That is exactly what we did.

We explained how and when we discovered that Philip was John's father. More surprisingly, John told us he never felt that Tom was his father, that there was always something missing. Choosing not to pitch fork the dead, he talked about how Tom was a good provider, but that as a father, he was like a bland pudding, emotionless and cool.

"Why don't you stay with us for a few weeks? I need to make a trip to California to wrap up some business."

"Maybe you could come along with me, we could get to know each other a little," Philip said in a caring and compassionate way. John eyed Philip, staring at his hands.

John had quit his job, sold the house in Minnesota and didn't have a place to live. He now found himself without a wife, without a home and a new found father. His personal belongings were in storage as he had plans to travel.

John had decided to stay in a hotel for two nights, giving him time to sort out his thoughts…until he saw Francine.

"Who was that?" he asked as he spied a stunning Francine walk by.

"That is our resident British princess/Greek Goddess," Philip quipped.

"She's baby Jackson's mother."

I went on to explain Francine's circumstances, the baby and the difficulties she's had losing Jackson and starting a new life in Arizona. John was quite taken with her beauty.

Carolyn was in the pool and Mitch was sitting in a lounge chair nearby, under a towering palm and joined by Doug and Sumana who had called a truce, acting again like love birds. All were quietly sitting there awaiting the arrival of the quail, as Carolyn had made a trail of sunflower seeds, bread and crackers extending from the garden to the edge of the pool.

Each day Carolyn had made the trail longer, baiting them to eventually reach the edge of the pool where she'd be floating on her raft, like a huntress stalking her prey.

The quail showed up as planned and walked single file across the concrete deck eating the mixture, like fire burning the end of a lit fuse. Carolyn sat quietly on her raft, the dogs asleep at her side. One quail finally made it over to Carolyn and they stared at each other, eye to eye.

All of a sudden, the quail jumped onto Carolyn's lap and she flung her right arm over the concrete edge of the pool to stop herself from flipping backward. She startled Thunder and Rocket from their siesta and both fell into the water, their little legs paddling for their lives. When she went to reach for them, Carolyn flipped over hitting her head on the edge of the pool scraping her face.

The agitated water was mixed with Carolyn's frantic cries, the dogs barely keeping their heads clear and a water soaked quail, wing up, floating on its side.

Within moments Mitch had jumped in and fished out Carolyn and the dogs. The quail went limp and Mitch determined it had died from fright. The dogs were a little shaken up, but then again, they were Chihuahuas, we couldn't tell the difference.

Mitch was excited. He finally got to dust off his make-up kit. We left John and Francine alone at the house and the rest of us chaperoned our injured quail whisperer to the hospital.

The ER staff, now used to our traveling in a pack, knew us on a first name basis. Carolyn managed to break her right arm in two places and a hard cast was ordered. They'd determine later if pins were necessary.

Carolyn remained poolside for a few days and could only enter the pool at the shallow end for walking or leg exercises and only if Mitch was in the pool with her. She promised to stop luring the quail.

We all had appointments with specialists one day and showed up as a group at the health center, looking as if we were going to hang out at the mall.

Doug was placed on a new pharmaceutical cocktail that'd take another ten days to reach full efficacy. We couldn't wait to see the outcome of that.

Sumana had a few tests and was diagnosed with Parkinson's disease, an affliction that would try to steal her creative spirit and would lose. Gary had some blood work and was given a clean bill of health for now. He'd require one more follow-up visit before they'd say he was cancer free.

I told the ophthalmologist that I'd be getting a second opinion in Boston and that I'd see them next year – maybe. It turned out that Carolyn sustained a spiral fracture in her arm and surgery was required to insert pins. Mitch dropped some poundage and his blood pressure was good, so he walked away with a new medication regimen and clear passages to his heart.

As the days went by, Doug, without delusions, spent a great deal of time sitting in the rocker listening to music, wearing headphones and with a drum tapping hand to thigh, he looked like an adolescent trying to escape parental oversight.

Sumana spent most of the time in her art studio painting lofty water colored landscapes for her new found art friends in Sedona and looked forward to an art show next June.

Mitch, keeping one eye on Doug, spent most of his time watching over Carolyn and Jackson Jr., while Francine was taking classes for her nursing license. Philip and John were spending time getting to know each other and planning their trip to California.

The date for our departure to Boston was approaching. I spent most of my time reading, looking at family photos and journaling, not knowing if I'd ever see again.

Scenic photography books from Banff, Ireland, Italy, England, Canada and Alaska, brought me a great deal of pleasure.

I took an anti-anxiety pill to quell the drama and played with baby Jackson who gave me belly laughs. My friends, who loved me unconditionally, took care of me in every way they could.

The night before Gary and I left for Boston, we had a dinner party. Gary baked his Sunday bread, Carolyn with her broken arm managed to bake two apple pies with walnuts and raisins. Philip cooked lobster tails and scallops on an outside grill and Sumana made her spinach quiche, with Swiss cheese, apples, walnuts and sausage.

Mitch roasted a turkey, complete with filling and baked butternut squash, corn, peas and mashed potatoes. We used Carolyn's fine china and Gary's crystal wine glasses that had belonged to his mother.

We hadn't realized it until sitting down that we created a Thanksgiving feast, possibly the last I'd ever see. It was the first time I ever ate turkey while breaking out in a sweat.

We talked about Peaceful and how poverty stricken we were. Some of us worked, and some attended the University. Tom and Gary had just completed their undergraduate degrees and were working as bartenders in the city.

I had completed my nurses training and was working part-time at a health clinic. Philip was doing sporadic carpentry work and Roger worked at a local seafood market.

Sumana and Doug worked different shifts at a foster school for delinquent youths and Carolyn baked pies, selling them to local restaurants and grocery stores.

Mitch was a full-time day student and at night worked as a short order cook in a local greasy spoon. While we managed to have an income, it was a very small one.

Carolyn stayed at home and tended a large garden we had in the back yard, which yielded a large crop of vegetables, including lettuce and potatoes. We also had a few layers that would yield two dozen eggs a month. Roger would bring home unsold seafood from the market, such as shark, scallops, crabmeat and halibut. The seafood and vegetables became staple foods and when supplemented by Gary's fine baked bread, Carolyn's pies and the greasy fries that Mitch would bring home, we were in pretty good shape most nights.

We all managed to eat at least one meal a day at work and did our best to keep the cost of food down, as we had limited funds. Tom and Gary kept us in supply of bar nuts.

The memory that dominated the discussion most was the night of Sumana's accident.

She had volunteered to go down to the market to get ice cream for us and decided to take her ten speed bike. When she got to the bottom of the hill, her left foot slipped out of her flip flop and went directly into the spinning spokes of her front tire, stopping her bike cold and causing substantial damage to her left foot. She flipped over the front of the bike, did a few somersaults and landed in the street face down, scraping her chest, stomach and face on the pavement.

Sumana managed to walk to the market and ask for help. We didn't have a phone so there was no way for the store owner to reach us.

After a considerable amount of time passed, Doug drove down to check on her and was told she had been taken to the hospital by ambulance.

Within the hour we joined her at the hospital where they placed a cast on her broken foot and bandaged her wounds.

Sumana playfully placed her left foot up on the table for all to see that she still had the scars from that night. She hasn't ridden a bike since.

Peaceful was an old house with no insulation in the walls. The first thing we did was to gut the exterior walls made of plaster and slats that had been there since the house was built in the 1800's. This was a dusty affair.

In one room we found old apothecary bottles piled up inside a wall, delivered by stagecoach. One bottle was bright blue in color with the cork stopper still in place. It had a skull and crossbones embossed into the glass, signifying that it contained a poison.

We found a pickaxe lying on a rafter, where someone had laid it over one hundred years before. And next to the axe were large empty brown whiskey bottles, signifying that someone had a good time.

Before adding insulation and new walls, we updated the electrical wiring. We found that squirrels were nesting cozily in the ceilings just above our heads.

We then added insulation and drywall, painting them in rainbow colors of pastel blues, pink and yellow. By this time we were exhausted. Then the bees came.

We searched but could never find the nests. First there were the yellow and black fuzzy bumble bees and then came the wasps. Every day without fail, they'd show up around four o'clock to go back to their nests.

They would buzz around all of the windows, fly across the living room and kitchen and then disappear when the sun set and only after they drove Carolyn insane. Carolyn didn't like bugs.

One day when Carolyn was alone at Peaceful, she ventured up to the attic to find something. What she found was a wall covered with and swarming with termites. She sucked them up in the vacuum cleaner, to no avail, as they just kept on coming.

She then searched the phone book for a reputable bugologist and hired him to treat the house for termites. Finally, with help from the bug man, Roger and Philip found the bee nests and Carolyn and the bees were set free.

Problems with the house renovations continued.

The heat and hot water system needed replacing, kitchen appliances broke and toilets refused to flush. The owner was running out of cash.

Living at Peaceful was a learning experience. We learned never to buy an old house and renovate it. The experience brought back good memories though, but we cringed when thinking about all the work we had done. Despite that, we never did complete the house and instead the owner sold it 'as is' to the first idiot to make him an offer.

Six months later, in July of 1970, we scattered to all parts of the country, taking what we learned into a new decade and new beginnings.

8

By the time Gary and I arrived in Boston, the tears would not stop flowing from my eyes. It was all so surreal; I felt small and insignificant, walking around the city like a robot, devoid of feeling.

In usual Gary style, we wined and dined and took in a show. We went to the science museum and the aquarium and drank Irish brew at an Irish café.

The second opinion was the same as the first, but they suggested I have the surgery soon, as further delays would result in increased symptoms. The dizziness had already begun, so I scheduled the surgery the following week in Boston.

The day before the procedure I spent the morning at the JFK Library, ate lunch along the water's edge and looked at family photos, possibly for the last time.

I spent a long time in front of the mirror, taking in the memory of my face, and cut my hair short to manage it more easily. I shopped as if there *was* no tomorrow, buying things I could ever possibly want or need, including a fur coat for the cool January nights.

I stayed awake all night reading a true story about the life of a man who coped with horrid adversity…yet his story came out well in the end. And gaining strength from his exploits, I was able to face my fate in the early morning hour, as if I were a prisoner on my way to an execution.

Before heading to the hospital, Gary and I made our way to the top of the hotel to watch the sun rise. He sent me into the operating room with a few pearls of wisdom: first reminding me that no one gets out of this life alive and second, that whatever happens, to remember they can't kill me and they can't eat me.

He reminded me again of our beautiful home with loving friends ready to take care of me… that I was financially secure and had good overall health. We talked about my son John and how our relationship warmed with the changes he had made in his life.

Gary reminded me that I was free, living in a country where we could reasonably expect good food and good health care, a time for me to count my blessings, reach into my gut and find the same strength that sent me trekking across the country alone at the age of 18 in search of a dream.

These were my thoughts as I went under the knife.

I could hear the nurse calling my name. The surgery was over and I was still groggy from the anesthesia. Both eyes were bandaged and a ceiling of darkness hovered above me underneath my eyelids. The gurney was noisy as they rolled me into the recovery room where the nurse helped me to sit upright.

When I was a nurse, I remembered the many patients who thanked me for the care I had given them. Since I worked in the ER, it became a rote affair. Some people would return with flowers and a card, others never made it home.

But one never truly appreciates the care they receive from a nurse until they are lying flat on their backs, almost dead, staring upward. Then they are elevated to the status of angels.

That was how I felt on that day at the hospital. My nurses had been sent to me from God.

It would be a few days before the bandages could be removed, so Gary took me back to the hotel, where we drank champagne to celebrate my bravery. Our room was filled with the scent of fresh cut roses; smelling like the color red.

He arranged for the hotel Chef to prepare my favorite meal of eggplant parmigiana, breaded and deep fried in olive oil, under mozzarella cheese and tomato sauce, served with spaghetti and red wine; chocolate cheese cake for desert.

In the morning I awakened to the smell of the chocolates Gary had placed on my nightstand while I was asleep. Who was this little man with a heart of gold?

The next few days were spent at the hotel, walking around in my dark world, bumping into furniture and holding onto the toilet to make sure I didn't fall off.

When the bandages were removed I learned that the vision in my left eye was blurry. The vision in my right eye was gone. It would never see the light of day again.

We returned to Arizona and the vision in my good eye continued to improve. For the first time I received my own prescription for marijuana, as it was critical for me to rest my good eye every few hours and to get a good night's sleep.

Things were happening at the ranch, so I had to move on from this drama to help take care of Carolyn.

Carolyn had the surgery to insert pins in her arm to hold the healing bones in place. She was in a great deal of pain from the arthritis in her hips and was smoking a lot of pot.

When not bedridden, she used an electric wheel chair to get around.

Her daily pool ritual was suspended for a while and we made a small bed on her footrests so Thunder and Rocket could be nearby without getting their little legs or paws stuck under the wheels.

We each took a shift caring for Carolyn; even Doug stepped up to the plate, reading her favorite books.

Had we not been there, Carolyn would most likely have gone to a nursing home to recover. But then again, had we not been there, there'd be no pool.

One night at dinner Gary showed us a stack of letters that arrived in the mail from family members seeking a home for their elderly relative. For some reason, word on the street portrayed us as a commercial enterprise open for business. It took several hours to craft a generic response letting them know this was a family home.

It was just the beginning.

We noticed people walking down the street and on the sidewalks adjacent to the house, staring in our direction as if coming upon a crime scene.

The letters continued to arrive daily and we worked to make certain families received a written response.

About two weeks later, a man arrived at our door, dressed in a suit like he was going to a Sunday sermon. We were all there when the door opened: Carolyn sitting in her scooter, arm in a cast with Thunder and Rocket tucked in, Doug using a walker as his feet hurt that day, I was still wearing a patch over my right eye and Gary's eye was looking up the road for crows more intensely than it ever had before.

Sumana's hands, arms and torso were now beginning to shake noticeably and Philip just looked plain exhausted having just returned from California.

Francine and John, young and fresh wearing decent clothes, looked like our social workers. We were a sight to behold.

When the man identified himself, Gary allowed him to enter the house.

It turned out he was an investigator working for the state of Arizona and was there to ask questions about our living arrangements. As if written on a bathroom wall, somehow he too got word we were a commercial operation and wanted to know why we were operating without a state license.

We turned this over to Gary who explained we were not a commercial enterprise, that we were friends who had lived together once before and were living together again.

He added that we were able to live here independently and took care of each other. Gary spoke about the variances filed when the houses were joined, that it was a residential property in a residential zone, that no one pays for or receives any money for services rendered.

The gentleman had commented that several local residents saw our 'Wrinkle Ranch' sign through the glass surrounding the front door near the foyer and assumed we were a business. The gentleman thought it was best to take down the sign. In fact, he demanded it.

Gary laughed and stated, "This is a private residence and the state has no authority to enter our home and tell us to take a sign down that is in our hallway inside of our home. That, my friend, is a violation of our constitutional right to privacy. If we choose to hang a sign inside our home calling it, 'Your Aunt Matilda's Best Little Whore House in the USA', we can do that too."

"People will continue to see the sign and assume you're open for business," the man said.

"If people are peeking in our windows, that's a police matter. We can't control what people do or what they believe," Gary retorted.

"There's no reason for anyone to file a complaint. This is a problem your office will need to address. We're not taking down our sign."

Gary then politely asked the man to leave.

"Are you a lawyer?" asked the man.

"I am," Gary replied.

"Are you licensed to practice in the state of Arizona?"

"I am," Gary replied.

"The problem is, we've never seen people in this type of living situation before," the gentleman added.

"I can't help you or your agency overcome short sightedness," Gary said. "Your demand is way out of line," Gary said as he walked to the door.

Gary made copies of the gentleman's identification and wrote the name of his supervisor on a business card. He made a call to complain about the unreasonable demand made by the investigator. The supervisor understood and apologized.

Gary later filed a complaint with the local Sheriff's Department to report that neighbors were peeping through our windows. They agreed to step up patrols in the area.

We were all impressed with our resident jurist and sang his praises the remainder of the day. Gary came to dinner wearing boxing gloves, shorts and sneakers, punching and jabbing like a fighter entering an arena. He almost pulled it off, had he not resembled a kangaroo having a seizure.

Later that night our neighbor Marty stopped by to tell us that his wife, aged eighty, had a stroke and needed nursing care in a medical facility. Hospital social workers had told Marty that the only nursing home bed available for his wife was in the state of Montana. He added that if she were to go there, he'd never see her again.

He asked if she could move in with us.

Gary reminded Marty that we were not a nursing home, that we were friends living together as friends. There were limits in our ability to care for someone who truly required skilled nursing care in a residential setting 24/7.

We were powerless to help and saddened for Marty.

With eyes to the pavement, Marty walked slowly back to his house looking dejected. The next day there was a sale sign on his front lawn.

Another round of news reports discussed the shortages of alternative housing facing aging baby boomers. While it didn't seem possible, the bean counters projected that it could take close to 1.2 million beds in each of the 50 states to care for those requiring skilled nursing care or assisted living housing. Even a hefty mortality rate would do little to reduce those numbers.

Until more facilities were constructed and group homes approved, the contingency plan would involve sharing beds around the country, similar to Marty's situation.

The federal government issued emergency funds to each state specifically to award contracts to construct new buildings or to modify older facilities all across the nation. The search was on for abandoned buildings in urban and rural areas that would benefit from developing the necessary infrastructure and construction the funds would bring.

It was a good time to be an architect.

While we were in Boston, Philip and John spent time together in California and discovered they had a lot in common. John's interest in building design was rekindled.

They decided to undergo the necessary blood tests to establish paternity and put the matter to rest once and for all. The tests came back confirming that Philip was in fact John's biological father. While happy for both Philip and John, resolution of the matter drove me into a period of melancholy, still punishing myself for not knowing.

But, it all worked out in the end.

What mental anguish John had suffered these last few months adjusting to a new father was about to be made up in a rather profitable windfall.

"Are you going to make another speech Philip?" Doug asked when Philip asked us to sit down for a talk. For some reason Doug hated when Philip hammed it up.

"I wanted to let everyone know that I've given John my house in Malibu Beach and he'll also be running my business that'll pass on to him when I die. He can have all the headaches and the profits. Once these new government contracts are issued there'll be plenty of business. I'll stay on as the primary until he gets his license to practice."

Philip had given John a new beginning and it helped to reconcile our differences. John didn't waste any time pulling together his plans and was gone within a week. I thanked Philip for what he had done for our son and for the first time in years was happy for John.

Gary was becoming engrossed by the letters arriving at the house daily and enlisted Doug and Sumana to help. Mitch was spending most of his time watching over Carolyn who was still recovering from her fractured arm and Philip was busy with paperwork. I had been spending more time watching Jackson, Jr. while Francine was finishing up her classes. And then the dogs barked.

This time they went out of control when an army of people approached the house. When the door opened we were greeted by a live news crew from New York wearing dark suits and a sheen of sweat on their faces. A lone reporter identified himself and approached Gary, who positioned himself in front of our pack.

They were there to do a story about the 'Wrinkle Ranch' that included an interview and a tour of the house.

Gary felt blindsided and asked the crew to leave. He told them to come back another day after submitting a list of questions in advance; that we'd decide as a group if an interview will take place.

We weren't interested in having our faces plastered on the television daily for a month and instead elected Gary to be our spokesmen.

Sumana was becoming more conscientious of her appearance due to an increase in her tremors and wanted no part of an interview. Carolyn was tired and looked pitiful sitting in the scooter with a cast on her arm.

And I still had the bandage on my right eye and held my arm out when making a right hand turn in the house. All of us agreed it would be media suicide to allow Doug to speak in front of the camera, fearful of what he might say.

Two days later they returned, cameras on shoulders, microphones in hand. We set up a place on the lanai out back in the hot sun to guarantee a short visit.

However, just before show time, they were whisked away to investigate another developing news story nearby that trumped ours.

It was reported that authorities arrested a woman for abandoning her elderly father who was found sitting in his wheelchair on the doorstep of a nursing home. He was wearing a sign around his neck that displayed his name and social security number. He was unable to speak due to a stroke and was deaf.

It took two days for the staff to realize he wasn't part of their flock. Like gumshoes with tunnel vision in a 1940's film noir, they tracked down the inconsolable daughter at her wits end, from prescription bottles found in his pockets.

The woman's life then spiraled out of control in a way she hadn't planned.

Her father had required specialized nursing care, but the home based health services were short staffed and booked solid despite the triage process. At least three times a week she took her father to the emergency room to obtain the required catheterization and replacement of his feeding tube and although he was on a waiting list, no beds were available for six months.

Her arrest and subsequent jail time made it possible to finally get him the care he needed when he became a ward of the state. But this didn't bode well for her fifteen year old grandson, also living in her home, who had to be placed in foster care until she finished her sentence.

The irony of course is that the state now foots the bill for all three of them and she can finally take some long overdue naps and a break from all the chaos.

Back at the ranch, Gary reviewed the questions and the news crew set up in the backyard as planned. The front area of the house was surrounded by neighbors. Thunder and Rocket were sent to the solitude room for their own peace of mind and we perched ourselves front and center.

"How many people live here at the Wrinkle Ranch?"

"We have eight adult's right now, and one infant; our resident grandchild."

"When did you and your friend's first meet?"

"We met in California at Golden Gate Park in 1966."

"Are any of you related?"

"Well, two of our friends have a son together. But that's a new development."

"How can that be?"

"Well, that's a long story and a bit personal. But we're all just great friends - we consider ourselves family."

"Do any of you have family members living elsewhere?"

"Some have kids in their late 40's – but our parents, Aunts and Uncles are all gone."

"Do you provide medical care here?"

"No. We go to the doctors and hospital just like everyone else. This is not a medical facility. This is our home."

"Where did you come up with the name of your sign, 'Wrinkle Ranch'?

"We were sitting around a hot tub one afternoon and someone shouted, 'Hey, this beats sitting in a wrinkle ranch'!"

"How long can you expect to live here in this house?"

"We're committed to staying as long as we can."

"What happens if someone dies?"

"Then, I guess we'll have to bury them."

"How do you handle finances?"

"We pool our money and pay the bills, like anyone else would do. But trusts have been set up to provide for our future care."

"So, what do you do in case of an emergency?"

"We dial 911, like everyone else."

"Do you do your own cooking?"

"Yes. We also drive, shop, travel, repair our cars and care for each other."

"What happens when you can no longer do that?"

"We'll probably order take-out and have it delivered. There's a great pizza place down the street."

"How do you keep safe? Do you have a security system?"

"Well, it wouldn't be secure if I told you about it on national television."

"And why is that man dancing naked in the other room?"

"Oh, don't worry about him. He's from New Hampshire."

Heads turned to see Doug, naked as the day he was born, spinning in circles, arms stretched out. Sumana buried her face into her hands while Mitch and Philip directed Doug toward his bedroom, where laughter erupted from behind closed doors.

"Why does he do that?"

"This is his home. Haven't you ever danced naked in your house?"

"What would you do if your friends died tomorrow?"

"Personally, I would cry."

"What I meant to ask was who would live here then?"

"I don't have the answer for that."

"Well then how does one get into the Wrinkle Ranch?"

"By invitation only."

It wasn't long after this interview that Sumana received a call from the adult day camp saying they had a vacancy for Doug, where he'd go for five hours a day, five days a week.

This lasted about one month until we received a call from the Director of Nursing who spent a lot of time observing Doug interact with fellow campers. She suggested we have him reevaluated, as she didn't believe he had dementia.

Gary and Philip took Doug, along with his bag o'meds, to numerous specialists where more testing was done. At the same time, I was coordinating the appointments and making certain test results and doctor opinions were being shared among the specialists.

After several meetings, it was finally concluded that the Director of Nursing was correct. Doug was not suffering from dementia as we were led to believe.

Instead, he had a seizure disorder along with a slight flaw in his character that showed up in a personality assessment. A new treatment plan was created.

Transitioning him off medication would be challenging, so they kept him as an inpatient for three days before starting him on a new drug regimen.

Mitch offered his left testicle if they'd give Doug a lobotomy, but they refused. We all wondered what Doug would be like when he returned.

During the nights Doug was away from the house, I discovered that the milk glass was absent from the kitchen sink. I began to wonder if Doug had an allergy to milk.

The doctor's confirmed my suspicions. It turned out he *was* lactose intolerant and is now prohibited from drinking milk or eating other dairy products as doctors believed this may have affected his behavioral health.

All of us were growing more concerned about Sumana, as we could see her daily struggles increasing. Her thinking and speech continued to be crisp, but the Parkinson's was taking a toll on her body.

She experienced some allergic reactions to medications that caused vomiting and hives, the ten inch wheel kind that caused severe itching. After a few weeks of this we were able to get her back on track with a new medication that helped to calm her movements.

Sumana was able to get more relief in the pool where the weight of the water added resistance, helping her to feel more in control of her body.

Carolyn finally had the cast and pins removed from her arm. Her arm was wafer thin and she required physical therapy to regain strength. I was able to get the exercises from the physical therapist and work with Carolyn every day to bring her up to speed. In time she could use her walker and spend more time in the pool again, something that brought her great happiness.

Mitch and I were still doing the shopping, but with only one eye, I tired more easily. As the doctors predicted, I had to rest my good eye several times a day to give it a break from the stimulus it received from the sunlight. I was glad that John was no longer in the house as I felt uncomfortable smoking pot in front of him. Despite any changes, he still had that bureaucrat thing going.

Gary was concerned about my not getting out of the house enough. So Philip, Gary and I started taking Ti Chi classes at the local recreation center. This was a good way for me to improve my balance, as I have been a bit more wobbly lately.

When Doug came home we immediately noticed a change in his physical appearance. He had gained a little weight, his eyes looked clear and he appeared tall, strong and confident.

He spent less time in front of the stereo and was more engaged with us, helping to prepare meals, feeding the dogs, helping Sumana and Carolyn and doing small chores around the house. He spent time in the pool with Sumana, one of the few activities they could share.

We noticed Doug was taking just a fraction of the medication than in the past and no longer taking sedatives. He had a renewed interest in his health, drank water instead of milk, walked with me and Philip in the morning and ate mostly fruits and vegetables. Philip was a little skeptical and waited for the other shoe to drop. But I was convinced there was a genuine change for the better.

This change in Doug came just in time, as Sumana began to deteriorate. She no longer painted or did any art work in her studio and we believed she was depressed. We shared this with her doctor who prescribed an anti-depressant that she refused to take.

Sumana kept telling us it was the medication that was making her sick. We took her back to the neurologist for another evaluation and did what we could to make her comfortable, but the constant physical movements and lack of sleep were affecting her mood. We offered distractions to keep her busy, but there was little we could do to prevent her suffering, when Mitch told us this story:

One night while he was on duty as a Paramedic, a woman had gone into labor - overdue three weeks for the birth of her first child.

The woman was in the early stages of labor with contractions two minutes apart. She had lost her mucous plug and all signs pointed to an impending delivery.

Forecaster's predicted a small snowstorm. But the community was stunned when a raging blizzard arrived that paralyzed the entire region. Shortly after arriving at the woman's house, rescue personnel were forced to stay there due to drifting snow that reached the second story windows of the apartment. City snowplows were snowed in and roads were impassable. Luckily, power and cable still worked.

The woman's doctor told her not to go out into the storm and relayed to Paramedics that the woman could only give birth by cesarean section due to an anatomical deformity. This would be a first for everyone.

When they summoned a birthing nurse, it took her one hour to cross the street. They notified the Coast Guard who dropped two Hospital Corpsmen on the roof. A basket was lowered from the helicopter and they asked the almost ten month pregnant woman in labor to climb into the basket to be lifted up through the dark of the night in the bone chilling wind, in white out conditions.

The patient, fearful of heights, had refused. If she were going to die, she'd take her chances with the men in blue and their medical bags full of drugs. Everyone waited with baited breath.

The two Corpsmen stayed at the apartment while the chopper crew responded to another home nearby to transport a child who had accidentally taken some pills. Had the woman been in route via the only chopper available, that child could have died. All were thunderstruck and believed this was a knock on the door from somebody's God.

The woman's contractions continued, her stomach rising and hardening every two minutes – the pain in its early stages. She grew more nervous and the sight of the raging storm, the flickering lights and all the people gathered in the apartment, was foreboding.

She then decided to sequester herself in the bedroom and asked not to be disturbed.

Alone now with growing contractions, pain and her private thoughts, she knew there was no way out, and fear gripped her heart like never before.

The storm raged on and for a full fourteen hours, rescue personnel, her husband and the maternity nurse waited for the road crew to arrive. A decision had been made to call out the National Guard.

They used a front end loader to remove the snow from the road, making way for a deuce and a half troop carrier loaded with six men. The storm now reached over three counties and the snow was ten feet deep and solid surrounding the ocean front dwelling.

When Mitch opened the bedroom door quietly to check on his patient, he found her propped up in bed comfortable and surrounded by fluffy pillows and a backrest. With arms and legs outstretched, the woman was breathing in slow deep breaths, touching her belly lightly in a trancelike state.

Mitch would have never believed it, had he not seen it with his own eyes.

The woman had stopped the contractions with the use of meditation. "Don't come out today", was her mantra, and baby did what she was told. All were relieved, but watchful, as if this were the eye of the storm.

The troops arrived and six men carried the woman over deep snow and transported her to the hospital where labor had to be induced, as she was locked up solid, giving birth the following day.

After that experience, Mitch began studying the uses of meditation and used it to help manage his own pain some years later.

He wondered if it could help Sumana.

Our solitude room was round in shape and insulated from noise like the sound proof booth in an audiologist's office. The floor was tiled and covered with a thick round Persian rug.

Large pillows covered with a brocade fabric were tossed about the soft comfortable chairs and one round coffee table made of oak. Bookcases lined the walls from ceiling to floor and were filled with items of spiritual significance for all faiths.

The room was a place to go when we needed time alone to pray, talk or cry out into the silent air, to whomever you chose; God, relatives, friends or pets you could no longer see.

It was a great place to meditate, a place to go quietly into yourself, into the depth of your existence.

Mitch began working with Doug and Sumana teaching them both what he knew about meditation.

He felt it was important to include Doug, so not to give the appearance he was excluded and for this to be something Doug and Sumana could do together every day, as it was helpful to both.

They each got approval from their respective neurologists and began listening to meditation tapes and reading books on the subject.

Mitch set one hour aside each day to sit with Doug and Sumana in the solitude room, where they would practice mindfulness. While Sumana's body was constantly moving, other times rigid, her mind, her senses and perceptivity were all sharp. She may not have been able to look you in the eye, but she could tell what you were thinking.

The goal of engaging in meditation was not to cure Sumana's Parkinson's disease, but to provide another coping mechanism.

Our bag of tricks to support Sumana was growing. We wanted to take her with us for our morning walks and she allowed us to push her in a wheelchair.

Gary and I would accompany her in the pool for one hour each day where I'd help her walk and we'd both hold her up flat to elicit a sensation of floating. Doug then took over and both would dally in the pool for another hour. Then, after lunch on most days, they would retreat to the solitude room.

The combination of the meditation and workouts in the pool helped Sumana to sleep, allowing her to be more energized during the day, which eventually led to a renewed interest in painting. She decided to do away with paint brushes altogether, switched back to acrylics and began using just her hands.

The abstract landscapes she produced, in vivid textured colors were astounding.

Although we never gave up hope, we knew that managing this disease was like putting a Band-Aid on a bullet wound; that Sumana would reach a point of needing a one on one nurse daily. So we did just that, not because we couldn't handle it, but because we wanted her to have the best care possible.

It took about six weeks, but we finally settled on two full time private duty nurses; each taking twelve hour shifts, five days a week. We'd provide coverage on holidays or days off and during times we were with Sumana in the pool and on walks, the nurse could take a break or eat lunch. So, it all worked out. Doug stayed by her side as much as possible and engaged in no more of his shenanigans.

We thought we'd have difficulty hiring nurses, given the state of the shortage of service providers, but it turned out to our surprise to be just the opposite in this case.

The services that usually provide care to elderly folks living in the community were booked solid - private companies or agencies that hired staff as employees.

But we found there was a glut of independent private duty nurses available – for a price.

9

The government began issuing informational broadcasts telling us that nursing homes around the country had reached capacity; that beds wouldn't be available until there was a change in facility populations caused by death or discharges.

Despite the clarion call from census data and failure on the part of the invisibles to avoid a crisis, the inevitable had finally occurred.

One option under consideration was discharging patients home or to a similar residential setting to free up beds for more serious patients. Another option to prevent the admission of new patients, was forcing children to care for their own parent. These became unpopular policies, spurring discord on both sides of the aisle. And not surprisingly, there was collateral damage in the aftermath of this tunnel vision policy.

Despite the unrest, the government forged onward creating a Parental Certification Program who's purpose was to match up elderly people, over the age 65, with their biological children. Those children would then be legally responsible for their parent's health, care and welfare. Sort of like responsibility *to* a child, but in reverse.

Children would be notified by mail of their parental duty and would be required by law to file an annual Parental Certification with their federal tax filing. If not, they'd pay an added 10% federal tax liability.

For those angels who already provide direct care for their elderly family members, and there were many, they'd receive a much deserved long overdue $10,000. tax credit on top of a $5,000. stimulus check from the government.

With electronic data available from genealogy records, Social Security Death Indexes, IRS data, birth records, passport information, Medicare and Medicaid claims data, matching children to their parents was a snap. These databases were a tie that bound everyone for eternity.

There were some children and parents who had been estranged for decades and others, who learned for the first time they were fathered by a different man. This gave rise to bad memories and unless intense coordination was afforded these special circumstances, someone somewhere was getting a surprise in the mail.

The government was mandating that children be responsible for their aging parents. Those wanting to terminate their relationship with the parent much like parents who can terminate their parental rights, were out of luck.

There was nowhere to go and nowhere to hide.

The certification filing would contain information to describe the parent's current living situation, their health status, driving status, home health services received and so forth. Medical and driving status would be verified through claims data and through the Department of Motor Vehicles.

Medical claims would give information to help clinical assessors create a profile to determine how that elderly person *should* be living, either independently or in some other situation, such as a one on one 24/7. The data would also show who'd be next in the nursing home line and matching parent to kid would help avert that admission.

If a parent was unable to live alone then the children were responsible for certifying that the parent lived in a situation that kept them safe and healthy. In some cases, if the parent *was* living alone independently, an inspection of the home was required to justify caretaking from a distance. If not, the child was responsible for meeting the needs of that parents' living situation.

While the overall intention of the policy was meant to serve the safety and health of the elderly, the policy caused a major upheaval and the fallout was enormous.

There were some children estranged from the parent due to abuse, neglect, drug or alcohol use and they were now being forced to take responsibility for that parent.

Others were removed from their homes at a young age, placed in foster care or adopted. Others had been given up for adoption at birth. In these circumstances, additional documentation was required to be attached to the certifications.

The government further mandated that family caregivers receive specialized training as licensed practical nurses and also have certifications in First Aide, Advanced First Aid and CPR. These certifications were to be filed each year with the parental certifications if the child was providing direct care for that parent. There was no opting out; no box to check if you were blind, stoned, disabled or homeless. It was a critical game of tag and you were it.

One of the main purposes of the policy was to offset the cost of long term care for the elderly who were eligible to receive coverage through the Medicaid program for both nursing home care and community based care. But that didn't matter so much anymore, now that there was no room at the inn and services were booked.

Many would force their parent to move in with them shifting from the warmer climates of Florida and the southwest to New England or another northern state, where the elderly would be chilled to the bone and house bound all winter long. Uprooting the parent would cause a glut in home sales; homes remaining empty selling at a lower price and reducing home values nationwide – part of the collateral damage.

In some circumstances, children could discover an unexpected windfall forcing the parent to *share* their wealth adding on that new bedroom or sun porch they always wanted. For others it meant financial suicide, having to give up one income when a spouse was forced to stay at home to care for the parent. This would hurt the national consumer index and reduce social security taxes - more collateral damage. Others may choose to disengage entirely and pay the tax penalty – it was cheaper.

And while the government offered stimulus funds to Colleges and Universities to ramp up their nursing and first aid programs, no funds were provided to beef up law enforcement to respond to or prosecute cases of abuse and neglect. After all, if they went off to jail, who's going to take care of mom?

But, there was no oversight for the quality of care the parent would receive. It was good enough that someone just took responsibility and possession, until a bed became available.

Then again, there were always those who just simply didn't follow the rules. Why get the training when you could just take dad to the ER?

It took a few weeks to digest this new policy and Gary did research to find more answers. We wondered what would happen in situations where an elderly person didn't have a spouse or partner to take care of them or never had children?

Gary found out that the invisibles drafted legislation to extend the responsibility to step-children, nieces and nephews for those who never married or had children. The fighting was fierce and he was doubtful that it'd pass.

We talked about it one night over dinner.

"So, this means that my boys will find out where I am," Mitch stated. "And does the law say I have to do what they say?"

"From what I understand, they just need to check in with you, make certain you're living in a healthy environment and submit their certification," Gary replied.

"What about Sumana?" Doug asked. "Can our daughter challenge our living situation?"

"All she is required to do is to submit the certification acknowledging the relationship and explain that there is a care giving spouse and 24 hr. nursing care at home."

"She could also add there are other responsible adults living in the home. The bureaucrats would applaud that."

"I don't want her here," Sumana said referring to her estranged daughter. Doug agreed.

"We'll try to do this by mail or phone," Gary assured.

"Let's just sit tight and wait for one of the kids to get in touch with us first."

"What would happen in a case where paternity was established after the fact?" Philip wondered thinking about his relationship with John.

"That'd be one of those special circumstances they talked about – but it sounds like they'd miss a few," Gary added.

Everyone just tired of all the government intrusion, so we decided to start having neighbors over for Friday afternoon luncheons each week. It'd be a good way to find out how others might be impacted by this new law.

Gary continued to do more research and found one loophole he kept to himself. There was nothing prohibiting parents from offering to pay the tax penalty for the kids under the condition they promised to stay away. He also began drafting legislation to submit to our representatives in Congress seeking to establish a waiver process for elderly folks living in communal situations, like ours. This would help us and others get out from under the thumbs of estranged recalcitrant children.

For a bunch of old hippies, we sure put on the ritz for those Friday afternoon luncheons. Mostly it was Gary and Philip who chose to use the china, glassware and table linens. Mitch was being fussy preparing hors d'oeuvres and finger foods.

Philip was in charge of the grilling and Carolyn and I were in charge of ice and drinks. Doug was in charge of sprucing up the house and setting up the music.

Most of our neighbors were in their mid-80's, and in good shape. Mid-day cocktail hours were a daily ritual for most and these folks were pretty well pickled. It only took one drink each before they all started griping about the new law.

One neighbor from across the street told a story about his own brother. All three of his children agreed to share him four months of the year which required him to crisscross the country by rail. It worked fine in the beginning until they found him dead in a sleeper somewhere outside of Atlanta.

One woman submitted paperwork in her home state to voluntarily terminate *her* parental rights in an attempt to avoid their malicious daughter from taking over her life. But, in anticipation of these requests, states placed a freeze on the process.

Everyone asked us questions about our living situation and how we went about finding each other. Gary and Philip told our story as some listened intently, while others pretended to hear but couldn't because the din of the background music combined with conversation trumped accuracy.

We got the sense that our neighbors admired the way we lived, but couldn't understand how we paid bills or resolved disputes. One man didn't allow anyone to touch his food and a woman wanted no one to touch her laundry.

As I listened to others, I knew with certainty I'd never be able to live with them.

There were mouth breathers who got in your face, others who were hard of hearing who refused to wear hearing aids and some who were just plain obstinate.

A few of the women seemed catty and one talked non-stop and even followed me when I left the room exhausted.

I later spied Carolyn stuck in a corner with my chatty friend. The woman complained about how her neighbor turned up his stereo too loud, that he sometimes kicked patio stones onto her Astroturf and let his bougainvillea grow over his front door. I could tell by Carolyn's droopy eyes she was bored, so I rescued her for a much needed bathroom break.

I still had no answer for what ingredients were used to bake our wonderful magic. But, I think it was unconditional love. Petty things never bothered us. At this age we had to pick and choose our battles carefully, saving our energies for the big stuff yet to come.

10

Sooner or later, your body will tell you when it's time to rest. Now it was Philip's turn. He came down with what we thought was a cold or virus. For a few days he suffered from a headache and one of his eyes was red, watery and swollen.

We learned shortly after that he was suffering from shingles that broke out on the left side of his head and face, affecting his left eye. This knocked our stalwart oak on his tail for months. He now carried his own bag o' meds and smoked a lot of weed to help curb the pain.

He stayed in the house for much of this time as he looked like an ogre and needed to stay out of the sun. We still took our walks in the morning with Philip wearing a large brimmed hat, like a cross dresser in an Easter parade, only wishing he looked half as good.

Philip took advantage of this down time to feast on much needed eye candy, gazing at the pretty day nurse, dressed in a navy blue scrub with glistening white Danskos marching around the house all day. In the evenings he helped Mitch with his memoir, editing and proofing what was written the previous night. He did a lot of research on the internet, watched movies and hung out by the pool with Carolyn, Mitch, Doug and Sumana, under the palm trees and out of the sun.

He took an interest in the garden and planted new flowers, something he always wanted to do and he helped Mitch and me with the weekly food shopping. With no vision in my right eye and Philip's seriously blurred left eye, we had one good pair of eyes between us when walking arm and arm down the store isles.

He'd pull me to the right - I'd pull him to the left, while Mitch pushed the cart behind us. We were 'Team Wrinkle Ranch' and were finished in an hour.

One afternoon Francine and the baby joined Carolyn and me while eating lunch poolside. She was done with her nursing studies and decided to take a trip. My son John had invited her and the baby to Malibu Beach for a week of rest and relaxation on the ocean.

It turned out that while we were busy taking care of everyday health dramas and keeping news reporters at bay, John and Francine were playing hide the weenie in the upstairs bedroom. My first reaction was to wonder if it was illegal and thought it rather peculiar. But then again, who's to judge? But as much as I chose not interfere with their business, Francine did take the opportunity to interfere with mine. She left me with an unsettling bombshell, that I wished she hadn't and it cast a dark shadow on her character that I'd not soon forget.

"John and I noticed that you've been spending a lot of time with Gary," she chirped intrusively in her coquettish way.

"So what. Why is that any concern of yours?"

"You must know by now that he's gay."

"What makes you say that?" I asked.

"No marriage. No relationships. He uses fine china and crystal. He's very neat, clean and very kind."

"Except for the china bit, you could say the same thing about Philip," I added.

I could feel my face starting to flush. What was it about this generation that got my panties in a bunch?

"Just be careful not to get too attached. We don't want you to get hurt," Francine said affectionately.

"It's too late and he'd never break my heart," I retorted with conviction. "I don't know much about gaydar and I'm a little slow on that uptake, but I think you're wrong. He's the kindest and most honest man I've ever known," I added.

"My point exactly," Francine concluded before she left.

Carolyn and I wondered if John put her up to the task.

Even so, we both couldn't ever think of a time when Gary had a partner, male or female.

"That doesn't mean he's batting for the other side," Carolyn surmised.

The sting of Francine's accusation left me hurting for days. Still, I knew Gary better than I knew Francine, so I just approached the issue head on.

"Francine thinks you're gay."

"Why would you want to know?"

"Well, I guess I'd just like to know."

"Why do you care?"

"Well, because I care about you and I think I'm falling in love with you."

"If you love me, does it matter whether I'm gay or straight?"

"I don't want my heart broken. Can you stop talking like a lawyer for just one minute?"

"Do you think I'd ever break your heart?"

"No. I know you wouldn't."

"But, to answer your question – I'm not gay and never have been. Francine's gaydar is off kilter."

"John thinks you're gay too."

"Then, if they both think I'm gay, it must be true, right?"

"I think I love you," was all I could say.

"I know I love you," was Gary's response.

"Are you gay?" I asked one final time.

"No I'm not. And I believe that is my misfortune. I've met some wonderful people in my life, gay and lesbian, who seem to be on a higher stratum than the rest of us."

"Well, I'm glad we got this out of the way."

"Are you a lesbian?" Gary asked with a smile. "You'd break my heart if you ran out on me."

"No, I'm not a lesbian."

"What can I do to prove to you I'm not gay?"

"What are you doing after dinner?"

"How about a little bingo?"

Falling in love again was an unexpected surprise. The passion that I thought was promised only to the young and beautiful returned to our lives in a way I believed impossible.

The birds sang louder, colors were enhanced and a passionate hue encircled my world. The love in my heart long dormant had awakened, as if for the first time.

We were no longer the salmon swimming upstream against the tide of life. We had crossed that finish line breathless and weary. We chose instead to nurture each other daily, much like a mother bird feeding her chick.

Francine arrived back in Arizona a few days earlier than expected. She had been talking with New Zealand and told us her father had been ill and was hospitalized. There was a chance he wouldn't make it and wanted to see his grandchild before he died. Francine's mother begged her to come home.

Carolyn never traveled much, but had always wanted to go to New Zealand. Francine asked her to go along; that perhaps she could help her with the baby. Carolyn agreed.

Philip made the travel arrangements while Gary and I helped them pack. Mitch kept baby Jackson occupied. The flight was long so Philip arranged for their return trip to be in three weeks, allowing Carolyn time to recover.

Carolyn was excited and happy to be taking the trip. I lent her my luggage, the carry on and a shoulder bag to help keep her organized. We'd never seen her so happy and energized.

It all happened so fast – hardly enough time to say good-bye. Before we knew it, the shuttle arrived and whisked them off to the airport. I wish I could've hugged her one last time, for it was the last time we'd ever see Carolyn again.

$\mathbf{P}$hilip received the call from Francine early and summoned John back to Arizona. By the time Gary and I returned from a day trip, John had already arrived at the house having taken an early morning flight.

With everyone seated in the living room, Philip began to relay the circumstances as Francine reported.

Carolyn had suffered a fatal heart attack earlier that morning, New Zealand time.

Francine's mother, a retired cardiologist, said that Carolyn got up from the couch, took one step and instead of moving forward, dropped to the floor in an instant. An attempt was made to resuscitate her, but there was no response.

That one small step took our Carolyn into another dimension.

Philip was grief-stricken and Mitch was devastated, both feeling that, had they been there, they would've been able to save her.

Sumana's facial muscles, rigid now with eyelids fixed in an open position, didn't prevent her tears from flowing like a waterfall. Each side of her mouth turned downward.

I went into shock for the first time, turning cold and unable to stop shaking.

They immediately covered me with a blanket, turned on the fireplace to bring warmth to my face and made me a cup of hot tea. So overcome with grief, we never thought of walking outside where the temperature was 108 degrees in the shade.

Thunder and Rocket were in their bed, curled up inside Carolyn's soft sweater she had left behind to give them comfort during her absence. And for the first time, we watched as four little quail sat peacefully in Carolyn's lounge chair out on the lanai. We wondered if the animals knew.

All of us cried, hardly able to believe what we had heard. Doug cried and held Sumana. Mitch, Gary, Philip and I held each other's hands and sobbed.

John sat nearby with his hands over his mouth, unable to find words, realizing I think, for the first time how much she had meant to me.

Carolyn brought such joy into our lives, with her funny little ways and her innocence. We loved her so much.

Gary faxed the necessary paperwork giving permission for Carolyn's remains to be cremated and shipped to the states. And like Roger and Jackson before her, Carolyn too came home to her family, in a box.

Needing time alone in the solitude room I cried out for Carolyn helping her to find the way back. A moment later a memory unhinged that helped me to find balance.

One night at Peaceful, Carolyn, Sumana and I spent part of the evening watching lightening bugs in the backyard. Carolyn didn't like any kind of bug, but Sumana encouraged her to stay. She agreed on the condition that she sat between us to protect her from an attack.

Except for the fireflies, the night was a sea of black ink and the piercing sound of cricket talk kept Carolyn guessing where they were.

Sumana held the stopwatch, Carolyn held the flashlight and I sat with my No. 2 pencil lined with teeth marks and a black composition book on my lap.

With this we were going to chart the dashes and flashes of light, like a firefly Morse code in the darkness and therefore, according to Sumana, we'd then understand the mating habits and flight patterns of the Western Russian River Fireflies.

Sumana said that each time a firefly would light up we were to track that with the flashlight and I would make a strike mark. We soon discovered that all the fireflies lit up at different times in ten minute intervals, after which they flocked to each other.

After the lighting frenzy, there would be total darkness, lasting another ten minutes. During this time, Sumana said, the fireflies were having sex, to which Carolyn replied, "But I can't hear anything except the crickets."

The cycle of lights on and lights off continued every ten minutes. We hypothesized that they used the lights to find each other, mate and then go back out with their natural search lights to find a new mate, to which Carolyn replied,
"I always knew they were sexy little buggers."

We also discovered that after a firefly would light up it then traveled rapidly - like a ricochet, into another direction, only to light up again, making you believe it was another firefly altogether. We hypothesized that this was some sort of mate chasing trickery or possibly a diversion to avoid an attack by another male when fast on the heels of a female.

Observations were keen and tracking precise. We were on the edge of exploration; bugologist's preparing to submit our data to the Smithsonian.

Things were going smoothly until Carolyn shined the light on her nightgown, and henceforth observed bugs of all kinds attached to her chest and shoulders like magnets.

In an instant, the flashlight flew outward and upward, cans of cream soda spilled on the deck while Carolyn ran screaming toward the river, stripping off her nightgown in stride; flip flops airborne, in one fluid maniacal movement.

She screamed one shrieking yelp but the bugs held fast, as did the bugs tangled in her long beautiful hair. Moments later we heard the splash of a cannonball-like plunge.

Roger came to the door. "So, was it a cricket this time?"

"I saw a Luna moth earlier," said another voice from a window.

It had been a long time since I thought about our firefly study. Was this a metaphysical contact from Carolyn meant to bring me comfort in my current state of sorrow?

Later that evening, Doug came to me and said that Sumana wanted to see me.

After sitting in the chair next to her bed, Sumana looked at me and was able to utter just one word – "fireflies". No other word could've brought me more happiness.

With that one word, I knew that Carolyn was near…and we were all comforted.

It wouldn't be long now before Carolyn's ashes were placed next to Jackson's. Philip suggested that the solitude room hold everyone's ashes where they'd be placed on a shelf for posterity. I could care less where mine went, as long as they weren't used to line the bottom of a monkey cage. But Philip had this thing about never wanting to be forgotten.

After much persuasion by Roger's family and Carolyn's father, she finally agreed to bury Roger at the National Cemetery in Arlington, Virginia. Carolyn later purchased a crypt in a mausoleum where she was supposed to be placed next to Harold. But after Jackson passed away, she told Philip that if anything happened to her, she wanted to be kept close to her son. So Gary sold her crypt back to the cemetery and donated the proceeds of that sale to the animal shelter. Now Carolyn and Jackson would be together forever.

We heard from Francine a few days later. Her father had also passed away and had been able to hold Jackson, Jr. just before his death giving Francine and her mother great comfort.

Francine would leave in two days to return to the states, so we made plans for a memorial for our beloved Carolyn.

Some of us wanted a quiet memorial, but Mitch and Philip insisted on having a huge blow out, complete with food, music and Carolyn's favorite wine. Francine sent a fabulous photo of Carolyn she had taken at the zoo standing next to a kangaroo. It was the perfect photo of Carolyn and we used it for the memorial.

When the opportunity presented itself, I confronted my son John about their thinking Gary was gay. I told him how intrusive it felt and how Francine had hurt my feelings. He apologized adding that he was just looking out for me.

In no uncertain terms, he understood loud and clear he was to stay out of my business. I told him I was disappointed with Francine's stereotyped characterizations of people, and thought it was ill-mannered.

While it was an emotional time for all, I had time to cool down before Francine arrived, but it would take time for me to warm up to her completely, if ever.

Philip was not feeling well. The anguish he felt over losing Carolyn and the preparations for the memorial were taking its toll. We all decided it was best to have the affair catered. We weren't in a position to make all the food and other preparations.

Philip was running a fever and just looked exhausted. He recalled that with all the activity, he had neglected to eat or take in any fluids. His blood pressure and blood sugar were lower than normal.

We gave him water, orange juice and some potato chips to help with his salt intake. As a precaution, Gary and I took him to the ER where Philip received a much needed IV for fluids as he was dehydrated. Other than that, he was fine. We took him back home where we made him a big dinner while he rested.

Mitch took Thunder and Rocket for a swim in the pool. He placed them on the raft, the way Carolyn used to, and pushed them around on the water. He stared at all the flowers Carolyn had planted and his face looked as if the bottom had fallen out of his world. Mitch spent a lot of time with Carolyn and we wondered how he would ever fill that void.

After dinner, we sat in the living room and tried to pass the time by flipping through magazines and reading. And then... the dogs barked.

We hadn't expected it so soon, but there it was – the delivery from New Zealand. Carolyn's ashes were inside an urn shaped like a box made of black and white marble. The driver used a dolly to wheel it into the house; the weight matching the heaviness in our hearts.

The top of the urn was adorned with a silver plate, tastefully etched in script with her name, date of birth and death. There was a piece of glass to hold a photo in the front.

Gary was quick to find a short white table stored in the garage and brought it inside so the delivery man could place the urn on top.

Philip was quick to find the tri-cornered American flag used to drape Roger's casket and placed that behind Carolyn's urn. Mitch cut six of Carolyn's white roses from her garden, placing them beside the urn in a silver vase.

Doug positioned the table against a living room wall, where it fit perfectly.

We felt like Carolyn was still with us. The nurse helped bring Sumana into the living room and Doug played Carolyn's favorite music album turned down low. It was very fitting - as if we were having our own private impromptu memorial. There was not a dry eye in the house and the delivery man let himself out quietly.

11

On the day of Carolyn's memorial, Philip answered the door and greeted a woman whom we had never met before. Her name was Nadine and she had recently moved into Marty's house kitty- corner from ours. She was holding a large peach cobbler, fresh baked from her oven.

Nadine extended her condolences, adding that bringing food was their way; neighbor supporting neighbor, a custom she learned as a child back home in the state of Georgia.

Philip was thunderstruck and embarrassed because he still had the shingles on his face and head. She put him at ease quickly when telling him she had suffered from the same thing a year before. They talked at great length about alternative treatments, herbs, supplements and magic potions to help bring about a rapid cure.

Everything about Nadine was peach. She was a tall, thin stunningly beautiful African-American woman with a flawless brown complexion with peach undertones that she accentuated with a hint of peach lipstick. She wore colorful silk blouses, accented with brown beads and gold jewelry that glowed behind the backdrop of her beautiful skin and short white hair. She was classy and had style.

When I met Nadine I knew with certainty she and Philip would be spending a lot of time together. I think that Nadine was a gift to Philip from Carolyn; she had shown Nadine the way to Philip's door.

When it was my turn to speak, I said this:

"Do loved ones who go before us, sit atop the clouds and look down
upon us deciding which one to take next?
If so, how they decide is the mystery.
Do they decide who had met their lifetime of pain?
Do they take the ones they miss the most?
When it was Carolyn's turn, I think I heard Roger say in that deep
baritone voice, "It's time to come home babe – I've been waiting for
you a long time."
And then he reached down, wrapped his arms around Carolyn and
plucked her from the earth forever.
And when we say good-bye to someone, we just don't say good-bye
to a person. We say good-bye to an era, to that time in our lives.
We can never go back.
Nothing stays the same.
Things will change.
I once had a friend named Carolyn.
She made me laugh and made my world a better place.
She was the sweetness in my world.
Always full of hope and sunshine;
She was the innocence in my world,
believing in everything and everybody.
She tried to open my eyes to the good in the world, but when looking
for goodness, all I could see was Carolyn.
I was fortunate to have her as my friend and family.
I will miss her deeply and will think of her every day for the rest of
my life."

Sumana couldn't enunciate words the way she wanted, but she
expressed her sorrow and celebrated her friend's life instead in a
painting of a beautiful landscape that she called, 'Carolyn's Way'.

There was a bright yellow and orange sunset overlooking a rose garden with palm trees. There was blue water that represented the pool and dots of colors that represented butterflies flying up to the sky. At the top of the sky in the center there was a peace sign that Doug had drawn and there was an angel in a white gown with long hair floating into the sky. The painting was magnificent and would adorn our hippie wall of fame forever.

Mitch told a very funny story that we had all forgotten about that helped lift our mood.

There was an old canoe turned on its side in the backyard at Peaceful. Carolyn had never been in a canoe before and begged Roger to teach her how to paddle. So the next morning, Roger, Carolyn and Mitch packed a lunch and some gear and headed up river. Carolyn was in the front, Roger seated in the middle and Mitch in the rear was in charge of steering.

The water was like glass. The bow of the canoe parted the water knifelike and Carolyn's long blonde hair, almost touching the floor of the canoe, swayed back and forth caught in a slight breeze.

It was one of those quiet mornings where the only sound you could hear were the birds awakening in the trees and the sounds of paddles being dipped in unison. The sun was just starting to peek through the morning mist, when all of a sudden, something whizzed by Carolyn.

"What was that?" she asked.

"A dragonfly," replied Roger.

"Do they bite?"

"No. They won't hurt you. Pay attention to your paddling."

They continued moving along, watching as the fish jumped up to catch their breakfast, watching blue herons sail between the water and trees and savoring the beauty of the baby ducks as they bounced in a long line behind their mother. It was going to be a spectacular day.

When all of a sudden, Carolyn took her paddle and swung it first to the left in front of her to divert the approaching dragonfly. She missed. Then swung to the right, and missed.

The dragonfly, the size of helicopter grew larger as it continued to fly, zeroing in on her face. The silence of the morning mist was about to be broken.

Carolyn swung her paddle again, this time in a half circle, twisting her waist with shoulders far to the right, enough so that her paddle reached the right side of Roger's head, smacking him with full force and over the side.

When Roger fell overboard, the canoe tipped far to the right causing Carolyn to lose her balance and she went in next.

Mitch, doing a delicate balancing act, with both legs straddled on each side of the canoe, managed to keep it afloat while the other two thrashed about in the water groping for the edge of the canoe.

"It was just a goddamn dragonfly!" was all that Roger could say.

They beached to dry off and then decided to eat their lunch early. Carolyn continued to ward off dragonflies and other bugs the rest of the day, but held a deathly fear of dragonflies for the rest of her life.

We'll never understand why bugs gravitated to Carolyn and why she responded the way she did. But we were glad that her remains were cremated so she didn't have to endure eternity with the threat of bugs looming in her space.

Nadine stayed long after all the other guests had left. She had worked for the federal government in Washington, D.C. and during those years, lived in Virginia. In addition to having a career, she had her own interior design business and many of her clients were incoming newly elected members of congress. Confident they would continue to be reelected, they'd have their home interiors redesigned and this would occur over and over following each election.

Nadine had a Master's degree in history, never married and had no children. Her parents were deceased and her father served in WWII, retiring as a Lt. Colonel in the Marines. He had suffered from Parkinson's. She was quite clear that he had died with it and not from it.

She'd taken care of "the Colonel" at home with the help of private nursing staff until he died of pneumonia. After that she sold her home and moved to the southwest.

Nadine had planned to move into an assisted living apartment inside a high rise resembling a hotel, but there were no units available. She decided to buy a house instead. She didn't like living alone but had run out of options. Except for some arthritis, her health was good.

All of us, most especially Philip, liked Nadine. She had a soft southern drawl and her voice spoke in a velvety fashion that was most pleasant to the ear.

In the days that followed, despite Philip's lingering shingles, he left the house with a spring in his step.

They spent time together visiting the zoo and attending spring training baseball games in Phoenix. Occasionally they'd drive up to Sedona or south of the border, but mostly they stayed home planning weekly luncheons as Nadine loved to cook and was a wine connoisseur.

Change was in the air and having Nadine around was like a breath of fresh air following Carolyn's death.

It didn't take long for us to notice there was something amiss as the woman we knew to be Francine returned from New Zealand.

Dark circles lay below the once beautiful eyes, which now appeared cold and unfeeling. Her lingering stares at Gary were puzzling and her hasty glances at Mitch annoying. She was impatient with the baby and often asked one of us to watch him while she napped. Her hair was stringy and unkempt; her skin pallor.

At first we thought it was from traveling, the death of her father or Carolyn's death, but this was not the case. The mystery was about to be unraveled.

Francine approached Gary and asked about the status of Carolyn's estate.

"There is no estate," Gary replied.

"You mean Carolyn had no money?" Francine inquired.

"Her money helped to fund our joint trust. Carolyn's remaining cash is in an education trust for the baby."

"Did she have any life insurance?" Francine pressed.

"No, none of us have life insurance. We're too old."

"She must not have been in her right mind when she funded that trust," Francine insisted.

Gary's face reddened, but he remained calm.

"Let's not pitchfork the dead Francine. Rest assured that Carolyn was in her right mind. We all were. And if she wasn't, you would not have asked her to go to New Zealand to help you with the baby, correct?" he added.

Gary could see the muscles in Francine's jaw line tighten; her teeth were clenched and her face red. Francine moved in, her face pressed up to his. The tension was palpable as Mitch, Philip and I silently walked into the room.

"Jackson told me she was very wealthy."

"Jackson was wrong," was all that Gary could say.

Francine backed away, but continued to push the issue.

"Did Carolyn have any kind of jewelry?" Francine inquired. Gary turned to look at me.

"No. Carolyn had no jewelry that I'm aware of; no furs, antiques or anything that could be of value."

"That's not what Jackson told me," Francine added, accusing us of lying, more or less; her eyes glassy.

"He told me she had a five carat emerald cut diamond, a four carat emerald, pearls, sapphires and a diamond watch."

"We never saw anything like that," Mitch added.

"Maybe she hid them somewhere," Francine pressed. "Did she have a safety deposit box?"

The questions rolled out, but Francine didn't get the answers she wanted. Her eyes stared out at the flower garden and then she quickly ran upstairs with baby in tow.

Philip said nothing, choosing to sit and listen to this exchange. We all stared at one another, wondering what to make of it all when a most serendipitous moment occurred.

Gary answered the phone call on the landline from Francine's mother. When he offered his condolences for the loss of her husband he added, "At least you'll be comforted knowing that he is no longer suffering."

Francine's mother sounded confused.

She informed Gary that her husband had not suffered, that he had died suddenly of heart failure the day after Carolyn passed away. He was perfectly healthy up until the moment he died; asking Gary why he thought her husband had been ill.

The color ran out of Gary's face when he called to Francine to pick up the phone. He took Philip and me into the solitude room and he asked Mitch to wait in the room and to watch Francine. Gary relayed to us what Francine's mother said.

"I'm getting suspicious. She's a liar," Gary said.

"What would you like us to do?" Philip asked.

"For now, keep your eyes on Francine. "I'm going to make a few calls," he added.

"Do you still have that paperwork from Paris?"

"Yes, it's in the same file with the paperwork from New Zealand."

Francine and the baby spent the remainder of the day upstairs in their room. But the saga was far from over.

When we weren't looking, Philip noticed Francine's long calculating stare through the glass doors outside toward Carolyn's flower garden. He read her thoughts like the parent of a teen-ager gone haywire.

Philip settled into his room for the night, but remained awake long after the others. As he expected, the security alarm was breached by an open door and he quickly silenced the noise from his smart phone before others were disturbed. Mitch heard the muffled sounds through his hearing aids. He then moved swiftly.

Philip and Mitch met in the hallway walking softly without a sound, barefooted on the cool tiled floor. They entered the living room where they observed Francine through the glass doors along the dirt border of the lanai, down on both knees. She was digging maddeningly like a prospector on the scent of that elusive nugget; both hands plunged into the crusted arid dirt beneath the rose bushes. Sand and multi-colored pebbles were strewn about disturbing a nest of scorpions.

"You won't find anything Francine," Philip said in a deep voice towering over the panic stricken woman. "Why don't you pull yourself together and come inside the house."

Francine stood up slowly, exhausted from the task, as the tips of her fingers unknowingly dripped blood onto the sides of her pant legs. The sound of the silence added salt into the wound and ended her prospecting days for good.

"It was all for nothing. All of it…for NOTHING! He lied to me. He lied!" Francine screamed running back into the house with Mitch and Philip fast on her heels.

Everyone in the house had awakened. Her high pitched screams bounced off the walls and ceilings. Her volcanic rage intensified, rising from a place where jealousy and betrayal had long festered and had now been aroused; a place where entitlement continued to exist, but remained unfed.

Francine was out of control. The guys cornered her while I scooped up the baby, moving him to safety.

"You need to leave now Francine," Philip told her in a calm voice. He stood guarded; prepared to take her down to the floor in a wrist lock if needed.

"I'm not leaving until I get what is mine!" Francine screamed while crying; her messy hair, wet from tears, clung to the sides of her face.

"Pack up your clothes Francine. You're going to a hotel. If you don't leave now, I'll call the police," Gary insisted.

Gary had upped the ante getting Francine's attention. The last thing she wanted was to be questioned by the police. She eventually calmed down and she and Jackson, Jr. were gone by morning. Gary paid the hotel for a one month stay to give him enough time to line up his ducks. He wasted no time.

The first call went to the authorities in Paris where they agreed to provide Gary with a copy of the autopsy and toxicology reports performed during the investigation into Jackson's death.

The next call went to the authorities in New Zealand, seeking the same on Carolyn. Those reports would not be available for two more weeks. The next call went to my son John in California.

"Why can't she stay with me?" John asked.

"I don't think that's a good idea," Gary implored.

"Why not?" asked John revealing an unusual and surprising trusting nature.

"We've got three dead bodies; she lured Carolyn to New Zealand under false pretenses and she went berserk when she discovered Carolyn had no money or jewels."

"That doesn't make her a murderer."

"She's no innocent, son. Two plus two equal four."

"She already got a large insurance settlement from Jackson's death. What's her motive?" John asked.

"That money could be gone by now. She's a gold digger, plain and simple," Gary concluded. "It's like an addiction. She'll never get enough. Bottom line – we don't want her around. And watch it, or you'll be next."

Philip could tell by the cadence of the conversation that giving up Francine was a hard sell. He took the phone.

"John, you weren't here for the last 24 hours to see her entire performance. This woman is bat shit crazy and we're concerned about the safety of the baby. Here's my bottom line – give her up or give up the business. You can't have both," Philip said, giving John an ultimatum.

There was silence.

"Philip, we were planning to be married. I just took out a life insurance policy naming her the beneficiary," John added.

"Well, cancel it if you want to live. Fax me a copy of the policy today," Philip said as he hung up the phone.

Just then, Philip decided to come clean with new information unknown to anyone else, adding that he was so busy with the house he forgot to share it with Gary.

The day before we left for California, before the house construction began, Carolyn told him about a plastic container she had buried in her garden behind the house.

It held Carolyn's jewels, money and a receipt from a cold storage facility where her fur coat was being stored. She wanted him to safeguard the items before the yard was dug up.

He removed the container and placed the contents into a safety deposit box. The contents, including the fur, were later valued at $90,000.

"This doesn't exactly make Carolyn a millionaire and still shouldn't justify Francine's actions," Gary said.

"Wealth is in the eye of the beholder," Philip reasoned. "So, I guess it all goes to the kid, right?"

"No. Not necessarily. Carolyn had already provided for the baby by setting up his education trust. I'll check the wording of the trust, but I believe any other assets she had at the time we established our trusts, belongs to that trust."

"Does Francine have any right to the contents of Carolyn's safety deposit box?" I asked.

"Criminals usually don't have the rights to any cache belonging to their victim before or after the commission of a crime," Gary added. "Besides, she's not Carolyn's next of kin; the baby is, as far as we know."

Despite the drama, we did our best to settle back into a daily routine, making certain to eat right, drink fluids, get enough sleep and take our daily morning walks.

Mitch was grieving especially hard and we included him in every activity we could. He spent a good deal of time in the pool with Doug, Sumana and the dogs, and was still working on his memoir.

The anxiety was causing me to have dizzy spells, so I made sure that someone knew where I was at all times in case I didn't show up for dinner.

Then those damn dogs barked again.

When we opened the door, we saw three men; one in a Sheriff's uniform, another wearing a blue pullover with the letters INS printed on the front. The third man was dressed in black and remained silent. They were looking for Francine.

Gary gave them the name of the hotel where Francine was staying. "What is this all about?" he asked.

"Did she have a child with her?" the Sheriff inquired.

"Yes, a son. Jackson Jr. is his name."

The silent one threw his arms up across his chest defiantly. We brought them into the house and out of the heat.

"The child's father died in Paris just before he was born," Gary added. The silent one became agitated shuffling his feet nervously and walking around in circles.

"That's not true," the silent man said in a British accent.

"Which part?" Gary asked in response.

"Francine is my wife and I'm the child's father. I've come here to get my son."

The man's first name was Patrick. He and Jackson were on the same faculty at the University and confirmed that Jackson's classes were at risk of being cut. When Jackson went on holiday to Paris, Francine joined him. Jackson and Francine had met at a faculty dinner and it wasn't long before he suspected they were having an affair.

Patrick explained further that Francine knew she was pregnant before she had an affair with Jackson. After his death she stayed long enough to wrap up personal business and then left for the states. It was possible that Jackson believed the child was his, but until we talked with Francine, we'd never know.

"We received a writ from an Inspector at Scotland Yard ordering us to take the child into custody and place him on a return flight with his father back to Britain," the Sheriff stated.

Gary took a moment to read the document.

"How do you know this is your child? Were you still in touch with Francine?" Gary inquired.

"Francine used her married name at the hospital and on the child's birth certificate," the Sheriff replied.

The fact that the child was born in the United States to British parents made it difficult to sort out his immigration status and the status of the parental rights of each were above Gary's pay grade.

We stood there stunned wondering what else we didn't know about this woman who managed to manipulate her way into our hearts and lives.

The thought of Carolyn going to her grave believing that Jackson, Jr. was her grandson was overwhelming. He was the child who belonged to everyone. We all fell in love with that little guy from the start, believing he was Carolyn's grandson. But it was out of our hands now - the whole sordid catastrophe.

My anger led to tears. Lies, fraud and possibly even murder. How did we not see the signs? How did we allow this to happen?

"Could I have the phone number of the Inspector you spoke with?" Gary asked. "I'd like to share some information with him."

Gary spoke with the Inspector to relay the events leading up to Francine's removal from the ranch. With new information, they'd open up a case to investigate the matter further.

But nothing at all was to come of it.

Francine, the drama queen, shot herself poolside. While her brains floated in the pool opposite sunbathing guests that morning, baby Jackson and his father boarded the plane destined for home.

What we believed was a love story turned heart breaking, was instead a frightful story with a tragic ending with tentacles that reached in all directions.

I had searched Carolyn's belongings for the book Jackson had given her containing Roger's letters, sketches and drawings. I was certain she'd taken it to New Zealand, but was now frantic as I couldn't find it anywhere. Gary asked the police to secure the book if located in the hotel room where Francine had been staying.

Understanding the sentimental value of the collection, police graciously returned it to us quickly instead of storing it in an evidence locker on the road to nowhere. It helped that the Sheriff's father had been a Vietnam Veteran and himself a Marine who served in Iraq.

A few weeks later I managed to find the courage to email the publisher in Britain. He told me he never met nor had spoken with Jackson; that the person who ordered and paid for the book was a woman by the name of Francine. The date on the order form was one month *after* Jackson died.

Nice touch Francine. How long did it take you to master his flowing script so that not even his own mother would recognize an imposter?

I said nothing to the others of what I had learned. Everyone wanted the book placed inside a shadow box on our hippie wall of fame. After all, it was a part of Roger and Carolyn. I cringed at the thought, knowing full well it was part of the bait that lured us in and took Carolyn out.

But when I looked into their eyes, Philip with permanent tears and Mitch's blanketed with sadness; Gary, Doug and Sumana's looked on with hope, believing that goodness prevailed over evil. Some things were better left unsaid.

We placed the book in a quiet spot at the end of a dimly lit coving, where the light would half shine long after we were gone.

12

The temperature in Arizona had reached 116 and it was time for another retreat to the mountains of California. We were happy that Nadine agreed to join us.

Doug and the two nurses stayed in Arizona to care for Sumana, who was suffering from repeated episodes of a sinus infection. She laid motionless for much of the day as her strength diminished and activities decreased. We spent time with her in the pool, keeping her afloat. She moaned with delight enjoying her morning soaks as the water, still cool from the desert night, danced upon her smooth dark skin. The heat of the sun rested upon her face.

Doug read books to Sumana daily and arranged the music through her head phones. Thunder and Rocket spent their days at Sumana's side, wrapped up in Carolyn's sweater, occasionally shaking from the house cooled air.

Sumana rarely spoke these days.

At dinner the night before we left for California, Doug dropped a bombshell.

"Sumana told me she wants to die."

Everyone, including Nadine, stopped eating and silence engulfed the room.

"When did she tell you this?" asked Mitch.

"Did she mention this to either of the nurses?" I asked.

"Maybe we should call the doc," added Gary.

Doug was unprepared for the inquiry.

"What's the law on that Gary?" Mitch asked.

"I'm not sure. I'd have to check. This is not an area of the law I'm familiar with."

"My mother used to tell me stories of old people, living long past their time, full of pain and suffering, long before the days when right to die and euthanasia issues were discussed in this country," Nadine told us.

"What did they do?" I asked.

"I don't know exactly…but people took care of their family and sometimes their neighbors too," she replied.

"Maybe it's similar to what some cultures did all across North America. When a member of the tribe could no longer pull their weight they'd cut them loose on an ice floe or if a family member felt they were a burden, they'd just walk out into the frigid air, lie down and go to sleep when it was their time," Mitch added.

"Well, there are no ice floes in Arizona," I said.

"Do you think Sumana's a burden?" Doug asked Mitch.

"No, I don't Doug. I'm just telling you what I've read and studied about the frozen north. All cultures, most especially tribal cultures, have beliefs about death that differ from ours," Mitch snapped back.

"Our country has to make a legal case out of everything," Gary added.

"Thank God for morphine," I added.

"Amen to that. My father was on morphine the last month before he passed on," Nadine added.

"Doug, maybe you and the nurses should call Sumana's doctor tomorrow and discuss this," Gary suggested to Doug.

"Maybe she's depressed again," I said.

"Maybe she just wants to die," Doug replied getting up and leaving the dinner table.

"Well that was a nice upbeat discussion," Philip said widening his eyes, looking over to Nadine.

"There's only one way to discuss those topics and that is head on – there's no avoiding it," Nadine added.

"Let's just make sure we heard what he was really saying," I added.

"So what was he really saying?" Philip asked.

"That he wants Sumana put out of her misery," I replied.

"You don't know that," Mitch said staring at me. "Doug said Sumana brought up the subject."

"I'm tired of trying to figure people out – do they really mean what they say or is it a cover up for something else," Philip said frustrated.

"I don't think we should listen to what they say. We should listen to what they do," I retorted thinking of Francine.

With that, we went back to our meal – discussion over.

We had an early morning flight out of Phoenix. Over breakfast Nadine told us she had spoken with Marty, our old neighbor who was now living in a small apartment outside of Helena, Montana. Marty's wife had passed away while living in a nursing home. He was out of money and couldn't afford rent or heating fuel for next winter and wanted to return to Arizona.

"You know he is a very wise man and was a big help to Carolyn before we came into the picture," Philip said.

"We have rooms available at the ranch," I said.

"He seems like a real likeable fellow. What would you say if we asked him to stay with us – rent free? Philip asked.

"We all thought Francine was a likeable fellow too," I added. "Look how that turned out."

"Marty is over 90 years old. He's harmless," Philip argued. "He'd probably just play the piano all day."

"You have plenty of room for that baby grand piano," Nadine added. "It's taking up much needed space at my house."

Marty had been a concert pianist and had left his piano with Nadine when he sold her the house and moved to Montana. This was a perfect opportunity for Nadine to move the piano along.

This was the first time we considered adding another permanent resident to live at the ranch. He was outside of our newfound family, but because of his history with Carolyn, we all felt obliged to him. Although he was older in age, his health seemed good and he could live independently like most of us. Philip would talk with Doug and get his thoughts, but everyone so far supported the idea. Besides, there was no place left for Marty to go – with the shortage and all. The thought of listening to live piano music in the privacy of our home was exciting.

I noticed that Nadine was spending less time at her home and more time at the ranch with Philip and the rest of us. Too soon to tell if they were a solid item, but I'll keep my one eye on that.

When we arrived at Gary's house in California thoughts of Carolyn, Jackson Jr. and Francine entered our minds, all here just one year ago. Reminders that change can happen fast. Where will we be one year from now? Six months from now?

And just like last year, the concierge, chef and cleaning staff were there. They had stocked our favorite wines and cooked our much loved meals.

Nadine fell in love with the house and took advantage of the on call massage therapist as she had arthritis in her spine.

With the use of the hot tub, massage therapy and smoking weed, Nadine was able to manage her pain while in California.

The last thing Mitch did before leaving Arizona was to join a writer's group. He met a woman named Candy and they continued to email and talk by phone every day.

Besides writing, they had a lot in common. She was a retired Sheriff from North Dakota and had just moved to Arizona.

Mitch was impressed with Candy and her hilarious stories of life in the ice lane. Like Mitch, she too collected rare books and just like Mitch, she too was writing a memoir.

Our mornings in California began with the usual wake and bake outside near the hot tub and our nights ended listening to Mitch relay the humorous stories about Candy's experience on patrol near the Canadian border.

One story told of a suspicious man walking alone in circles on the main highway through town during a cold snap, with temperatures at thirty below. Candy discovered he was from a neighboring city and offered to transport him to the bus station. She searched him for weapons before putting him in the cruiser, but while out on the highway, she watched in her rearview mirror as a five foot long boa constrictor wound its way up the wire mesh cage behind her headrest. Afraid it would crawl under the seat she pulled over and called for the Animal Control Officer to remove it.

The man had kept the snake warm by allowing it to wrap itself around his leg inside the bulky pants he was wearing. How she missed it during the frisk, she'll never know.

They shared rescue stories and divulged their rescue dreams: Mitch, plucking a toy poodle from a raging river and after breathing life back into its lungs, an applause rises up from a bus load of kids; Candy, sneaking up on a lone gunman in a bank, grabbing his throat from behind, her foot kicks out the back of his knees knocking him to the ground, where she is able to disarm him before back-up arrived.

Mitch had met someone special; someone who spoke his language, understood his thinking, shared in his ability to laugh at the absurd and at each other. Candy not only had the same hearing difficulties as Mitch, but was also a recovering alcoholic. There'd be no substance, including weed, in this relationship.

Mitch had found a true partner.

The first few days after arriving in California I suffered from a case of melancholy, struggling with the same introspection as when I lost Tom. Thoughts of every family member or friend who ever died stayed with me; constant ruminations about what it all means.

And then one day it hit me.

I was the keeper of their memory. Through me they were memorialized forever, good or bad. That was my obligation to each and every one of them. Sometimes the ruminations didn't stop, robbing me of sleep or the ability to live in the present and was a painful cross to bear.

Carolyn once said that storing her possessions in the trunk was like a death of a thousand cuts. She was so right. But on the other hand, I felt like my purpose in life had never been greater. Keeping their memory alive was an honor.

As soon as the reports on Jackson and Carolyn's deaths arrived in the mail, Doug mailed them to Gary by overnight delivery. Gary noticed that the envelopes had been opened, with Doug being the only culprit. He dismissed this oddity but couldn't help wonder why Doug never missed an opportunity to irritate people.

The authorities in Paris where Jackson died didn't do toxicology or blood testing.

After the autopsy, which showed damage to the heart consistent with a heart attack, they assumed just that, even though he was only 45. They hadn't yet learned of the large life insurance policy that would be paid to his supposed fiancée and hadn't checked with his physician to learn he had been in excellent health.

The report on Carolyn showed that she had a drug in her blood stream; one usually prescribed to patients with heart disorders. The coroner also assumed, because of her age, that she had suffered a fatal heart attack. But Carolyn took no such drug and never had problems with her heart.

Gary felt compelled to speak with the coroner in New Zealand and suggested, given the circumstances, that he compare Carolyn's toxicology results with those that may have been performed on Francine's father that same week.

We never learned the outcome of those results as Francine's mother insisted the coroner keep them confidential. We didn't have the heart to press on given the fact she lost her husband, daughter and future contact with her grandson – if in fact she *was* Francine's mother. We had reservations about everything now, when we should've questioned things sooner.

This latest development gave us permission to move on. It was time to let go of the matter as it would never be solved to our complete satisfaction.

13

The government Parental Certification Program was in full swing now. For parents and children who lived nearby or were a part of each other's lives, the outcome was routine. For others who managed to put enough dirt between them, and in some cases an ocean, their lives grew more exciting.

All around the country people were answering the doorbell where they found themselves face to face with kin they barely recognized. The savvy elderly asked to see identification; the not so savvy allowed them to enter.

In some cases there was a joyful reunion. In others, scabs were picked and ripped from the deep wounds that never healed. And in no time they were at each other's throats: the bastard who didn't pay for his wife's funeral, the bum who flunked out of college, the daughter who married a woman; the son who did time in prison and the children left out of the will.

The program caused a spike in domestic violence increasing police and rescue calls by 25%. Court cases were backlogged with failures to appear; Judges having to issue bench warrants for those children who lived in another state.

For the children who found their estranged parents living in squalor, they were now responsible for creating a better plan. The children who found their estranged parents living in sand colored haciendas surrounded by palm trees could rest easy for now - until the money ran out.

Those who were able to bury their discord reunited under one roof; like smoker's living with a vegan, destined to fail.

And like a bad flu, the certification program caused suffering for some, but for the many Americans who already cared for their loved ones at home, they breathed a sigh of relief.

One month into our stay in California, Mitch received a call from Doug who reported that Sumana was being admitted to the hospital with pneumonia. We packed our bags and returned to Arizona late the next day. We took a shuttle from the airport directly to the hospital where we found a distressed Doug sitting next to his near comatose Sumana.

"What did her doctor say about her wanting to die?" Philip asked.

"He said it wasn't uncommon to hear that. He gave her an anti-depressant, but she broke out in another rash," Doug replied holding Sumana's hand.

"I spoke with the doctor. He feels upbeat about Sumana's prognosis and believes they can get the pneumonia under control in a few days," I added looking Doug squarely in the eye to make certain he heard what I was saying.

"I gave the nurses a few days off – paid. They'll be available just before Sumana is discharged," Doug said.

Nadine hadn't known Doug and Sumana the way the others did and she excused herself from the hospital room, feeling uncomfortable and intrusive. Seeing Sumana lying there also reminded Nadine of her father who had died from pneumonia under similar circumstances. She met up with Philip in the waiting room a short while later and they decided to take a cab home. When driving past the ranch to Nadine's house they noticed a black car parked in the driveway occupied by a man and a woman.

"I wonder who that could be," Nadine said.

"I don't know. New York tags - might be a rental," Philip replied as they pulled into Nadine's driveway.

After Nadine was dropped off at her house the taxi driver drove his cab kitty-corner to the ranch. Philip approached the unidentified parked car, engine running with air conditioner going full blast. He tapped on the driver's side window.

"It's a little hot to be sittin' out here in a car, don't you think?" Philip asked the male driver. "Let's take it in the garage where it's a little cooler. Not really, it's a 300 degree sauna."

"Does Mitch live here? I'm waiting for Mitch. I'm his son and I need to speak to him about this certification thing."

Philip was shocked and wasn't sure what to do next.

"Well, who are *you*?" Philip asked looking at the female passenger.

"I'm his wife," she replied.

"Does my father live here? I have a paper here that says this is his current residence. We came all the way from New Jersey," he added.

The temperature was rising to over 100 degrees that afternoon. Philip had no choice but to treat them graciously. He sized them up as best he could: good looking, nice clothes, clean shaven, professional looking attire, no visible tattoos or bulges from under their suit jackets. In fact, he even saw a hint of Mitch.

Philip brought them inside, poured some chardonnay and seated them in the solitude room. He called Gary first.

"You gave them wine? What are you trying to do, start a drunken brawl?" Gary asked.

"What was I going to do? They don't drink coffee. They look like a couple of federal agents."

"Which kid is it, Bobby or Michael?" Gary inquired.

"I forgot to ask."

"Well, go ask. It might be helpful," Gary said.

Philip walked back over to the solitude room thinking what a great waiting room it made.

"What did you say your name was?" he asked.

"Tell him it's Michael," he replied with a smile.

Philip relayed the information to Gary who did some fast thinking about how to break this to Mitch. In the meantime, Philip served up some salsa and chips, chocolate covered mangos and more wine.

"So what part of Jersey you from," Philip asked.

"The Jersey shore," Michael replied. "We lost our house in the hurricane, but we're rebuilding now."

"Well, good luck with that. I lost the same house three times to the clutches of the Pacific."

"My father is on his way, right?" Michael asked.

"Yeah, he's on his way. He's at the hospital with a friend of ours, but should be here in a few minutes. So, what do you do for work?" Philip asked downing more than his share of wine. If there was a brawl, he wanted it to be a fair one.

"We're both federal agents," Michael replied.

Mitch took the surprise visit rather well saying that he expected this to happen all along. Michael was his youngest son whom he hadn't seen since the age of 7.

When Mitch arrived home we confined all three to the solitude room so the head bashing could be contained. After an hour, the woman came out and asked to use the bathroom.

"How's it going in there?" I asked.

"It's going pretty good," she replied extending her hand to introduce herself. "I'm Nancy, Michael's wife."

Nancy decided to stay and talk with me affording them some privacy. I told her about the Wrinkle Ranch and showed her our hippie wall of fame. We talked about the new certification program and how she had to track down her own parents farther north living in Sedona.

She added how Michael was estranged from his older brother; that the last time they saw each other was at their mother's funeral in the 90's.

She described the family as 'fractured' and hoped that Michael could establish a relationship with Mitch for the sake of their daughter, aged 10. I hoped so too, as Nancy seemed like a lovely person.

Finally, Mitch and Michael emerged from the solitude room with smiles on their faces, absent torn shirts or bloody noses. Despite Mitch's knee problems, they had the same walk.

Everyone was introduced and we spent the afternoon peacefully talking about the joys and perils of living life in Arizona and New Jersey.

Gary and Philip had been all jacked up for a brawl that didn't happen.

Nancy shared older photographs she had of Mitch's other son Bobby, his wife and their children, giving Mitch a total of three grandchildren. This was exciting news for Mitch – the timing was good.

We were all too tired from the early flight and the hospital visit to make dinner, so we took Michael and Nancy to our favorite watering hole downtown for dinner.

Michael and Nancy were free the next day, so we took them to the cowboy museum. Nadine joined us as this was a place she had longed to visit.

Making that long drive was always a reminder to me that we actually did live in a desert. I stared out the window watching tumbleweeds blow along stretches of gravel encrusted desert lacking vegetation, back dropped far off in the distance by tall dark mountains.

I had visions of the way the west must have looked in the old days; cowboys riding horses wearing wide brimmed hats under the scorching sun, with long arms holstered into leather saddles. The images looked just like Doug and I laughed out loud.

Occasionally we'd come across roadside stands selling gemstones, pottery or artwork made by local artists.

Shop windows were dusty from the sand storms, the wood siding dried and splintered from baking in the hot sun. There were places to buy cactus and palm trees that caught the wind above your head. The more I took in the sights, the more water I drank.

That's the funny thing about Arizona: you can drink water like a camel and never have to use the bathroom. It's a dry kind of heat, like putting a blow torch up to your face.

When we got to the center of town, Philip parked the car in front of the museum. We got out of the cars and walked up on the sidewalk, when all of a sudden we heard Nadine scream and fall to the ground.

All along the sidewalks there were replicas of very long snakes, some with their heads and bodies raised, that were cast in bronze crafted by an artist long ago. Unless you were familiar with the terrain they looked real and were shocking.

We had forgotten to warn her about the snakes and when Nadine became startled, she tripped, fracturing her right ankle. Philip and I took Nadine to the hospital and I listened as Nadine cussed words I never heard of and was frothing in anger over the incident.

Her ankle was broken in two places. This was a serious matter. At our age women cannot afford any broken bones.

Nadine wasn't angry with us over the accident, but instead, was angry at herself for not watching where she was walking. Philip felt responsible however, and made a plan to take care of Nadine day in and day out in the weeks ahead.

They grew closer and closer each day and knowing Philip I'm sure he took every opportunity to hold her beautiful leg and ankle in his hands or to sneak a peek up her shorts now and then.

Michael and Nancy returned to New Jersey with their completed certification form. They had plans on spending Christmas with the kids in Florida and invited Mitch to join them. He agreed and thought that Candy might like to go along too.

Things couldn't have been more perfect for Mitch. He was in good health, had a new friend, was writing a memoir and had just reunited with a part of his family. He was excited about getting to meet his grandchildren and for the first time since Carolyn passed away, his eyes were dry.

Sumana beat her battle with pneumonia and when she came home the nurses were ready and waiting to assume their duties. They were surprised to see a much improved Sumana, reporting to us that her eyes were more clear and alert than in the days before she was admitted. Even her doctors were puzzled, not understanding why they saw such a rapid improvement to her appearance and affect.

While seated next to Sumana I took notes on her new medication regimen. I noticed that except for the vitamin D, all pills were in hard pill form, not capsules. There were no narcotics of any kind; nothing to make her drowsy. So we began to wonder why, after seven days of being discharged from the hospital, Sumana shifted back to her almost comatose state, lying motionless day in and day out.

Her doctor told us that her decline was a manifestation of her depression and added a new anti-depressant that had little or no effect. Sumana hardly spoke and spent her days listening to music through head phones. We fed Doug, while the nurses fed Sumana. Doug kept a constant vigil by her side holding her hand. The house was silent. Even the dogs refused to eat and we were careful not to intrude on the special dance within this small unit of loving people.

Then, the following morning, on a beautiful sunny January day, with the night nurse sitting alert by her side, Sumana passed away quietly in her sleep. She uttered not a sound, nor gasped for a single breath of air.

We were in the kitchen making breakfast, ready to take it out on the lanai, when we heard the nurse call.

Sumana had been dead for too long and resuscitation no longer an option. Doug kneeled down and while bent over her tiny body, held her gently and sobbed uncontrollably.

As with all untimely deaths, the coroner had to be notified. They came to get Sumana and questioned everyone who was in the house that morning. They gathered up her medication, along with the vitamin D, to accompany her body for the routine autopsy and toxicology tests.

Nadine saw the commotion at the house and hobbled over slowly, her foot still wrapped in a soft cast, carrying a freshly baked apple pie. She noticed something queer about Doug's actions.

He sat rocking in a rocking chair next to the stereo system in the music room, wearing head phones and flipping through a magazine. If it weren't for the peaceful look on his face, we would have thought he was either catatonic or in shock. Mitch went over to check.

"Hey Doug, you okay?" Mitch asked while we all looked on. Doug just stared out past Mitch and closed the magazine.

"They're going to find out," he said shaking his head.

"Find out what?" Mitch asked in response.

"They're going to find out that I killed her," Doug replied.

The admission stunned everyone, including Gary, who was robbed of the opportunity to advise Doug that he should remain silent - law school 101. But, the cat was out of the bag and we all heard it.

Mitch's face turned a few shades whiter and upon standing he held onto the wall with both hands for balance.

"Did you hear that? Did you hear what he just said?" Mitch asked all of us. We acknowledged that we did.

Doug walked over to where we were standing.

"Sumana wanted to die. It was my duty to help her. I crushed up white sedatives and put them in her vitamin D capsules and slowly increased the dosage so she wouldn't vomit on the fatal dose," Doug admitted.

Gary suggested he not say another word, but it was too late. We were already in over our heads, pulled into the drama, witnesses against our good friend.

"Where did you get the sedatives?" a curious Mitch asked Doug, as Gary rolled his eyes and held his face between his hands.

"A prescription I had from last year was never canceled so I stockpiled the refills," Doug replied.

I could tell that by this time we were all feeling a little paralyzed from this alarming bombshell; an emotional abyss that prevented us from shedding a tear for our precious Sumana in the early hours after her death. Doug had robbed us of that.

His actions sent me into a rage for murdering his wife in our house, for admitting to it in our presence and for stealing away our Sumana. Then I did something that was not in my nature – a shameful act that I later regretted. I walked up behind Doug and took both of my fists at once and punched him on the back with every ounce of strength I had three times in a row shouting, "How dare you, how dare you, how dare you do this to our Sumana!"

Mitch, Gary and Philip didn't try to stop me and Doug remained still, accepting the blows as condemnation from me. This act allowed me to climb out of the void and feeling dizzy from the stress I was forced to take a sedative.

I turned to Nadine for guidance.

"Help me Nadine. I'm going out of my mind. I can't find any compassion for this idiot," I said to my friend.

"Who are we to judge if Doug believed it was his *duty* or not? He felt that Sumana was his responsibility and he'll need to *take* responsibility for what he did to her. There's nothing any of us can do or say to change the outcome. Just think about your friend Sumana. Her condition was not going to improve. Your precious Sumana is at peace," Nadine said. "Think about Sumana, not Doug."

And then, the thought entered my mind about the time Doug told us the story about his virus and how Sumana said that if he ever got it again, "she'd pull the plug." I thought she was joking, but I wondered if they had a pact. My thinking began to change.

How great a love must be, that one would risk going to jail for euthanizing their loved one. This was not a love between parent and child, nor a love between lovers in the heat of passion. It was a deeper love, one of commitment and promise above all else, beyond the self and beyond the scope of the universe or all the stars.

How could I judge his actions when I don't fully understand? These thoughts helped to put it in perspective, but forgiveness was stuck down deep in the pit of my gut about an inch below my broken heart, unlikely to rise any time soon.

Gary felt compelled to share what we had learned that morning with staff from the coroner's office who questioned us earlier. Before Gary got the chance, Doug grabbed the phone out of his hand and admitted to the person on the other end that he had killed his wife. The drama refused to end.

Gary just threw his arms up in the air and walked away. Police had no choice but to take Doug into custody and lodge him in the county correctional facility on the other side of town.

Doug told us he had planned to go to prison, adding that he wanted it that way. His life had been with Sumana and without her, his life had no meaning. He asked us not to defend him nor visit him in prison.

So we not only mourned the loss of Sumana, but the loss of Doug as well. He could be a handful at times, but he was our good friend and a member of our family.

I caught Philip alone in the solitude room with a mouth full of scotch and tears streaming down his face, crawling into a bottle to help him climb out of the abyss.

"I don't think I can handle this," he said.

"We don't have much of a choice," I responded.

"When we all agreed to live together, I never gave it much thought about how it was all going to end," he said.

"I know what you mean. Our circle is getting smaller."

"I wonder if Doug was stockpiling the pills before Sumana's health worsened." Philip wondered.

"He must have because he had to have a large quantity. But that's up to the police to sort out now," I replied.

"Our world is shrinking and I just don't know if I can handle losing you, Mitch or Gary," Philip added.

"So, is living anywhere else going to change that?" I asked sensing a tinge of regret.

"I guess not. I'm just so damn sad. I guess it'd be the same if we were all family, right?" Philip asked.

"We are family," I said in response. "Let's not forget that we are joint owners of a middle aged son. The longer we live memory of the others will live on too."

"Tell me you'll never die," Philip said looking into my eyes.

"Only if you tell me first," I replied.

We rested in each other's arms and thought about our friends, family, life and tried to make sense of all this pain.

"I wonder who'll get the tontine," Philip said as he stared at the leather encased box on the upper shelf.

"Doug said he wants to attend the memorial service for Sumana," Gary reported as he entered the solitude room reaching down for a swig of Philip's scotch.

He sat down next to me and held my hand leaning his head back on the couch. It felt good to snuggle between my friends.

"After the service, let's take a trip somewhere –get outta' Dodge for a while," Gary said.

"Where to?" asked Philip.

"Let's get one of those big RV's - drive up to the Yukon through Alberta. Then we can keep on going up the Alcan Highway into Fairbanks."

"Wow, you got it all mapped out, don't you," I said.

"You mean we can't use a VW Bus like we did in the past?" asked Philip. "We used to sleep five in there."

"That was before we needed food and a bathroom," Gary added.

"I always wanted to make that trip. It'll be good for all of us," Gary concluded.

"Better bring some bear spray," I said to Gary.

"All I need to do is run faster than you!"

"I'll run faster than both of you," added Philip

"We could use some bug spray," Gary added. "They got some big skeeters up there."

"So, where's the RV store? You fly and I'll buy," added Philip. "The only thing I want is a decent shower so we can survive in those tight quarters – could take us a few months."

Just then Mitch joined us.

"Hey Mitch, wanna' go to the Yukon?" Gary asked.

"Hell yeah," was all he could say.

14

Sumana's service was attended by a small gathering of our neighbors, along with friends she had met in the Tucson and Sedona art communities. We displayed the urn in Sumana's art studio where it was surrounded by her paintings; Thunder and Rocket curled up asleep in front of the fragrant flowers.

Then Doug arrived handcuffed in the front and flanked by two stiffened Sheriffs who, without talking, told us to keep our distance. Doug knelt down and began to cry softly, later growing into uncontrollable sobs.

"May I?" I asked the Sheriff as I approached Doug with tissues so he could wipe his tears and runny nose.

Doug began crying out the words, "I'm sorry, I'm sorry" as he looked up at each of us standing there. Gary found his compassion and as we watched, placed his hand on Doug's shoulder.

"Take it easy Doug. We don't fully understand it all and I'm not sure we ever will. We just want you to have peace," was all that Gary could say.

Doug knew this might be the last time he'd ever see Sumana's urn, artwork and studio. He knew this could be the last time he saw us – as he wished – a sort of self-imposed punishment for his final loyal act of love.

As agreed, at the close of Sumana's service, we got outta' Dodge and were glad we did. Before leaving Philip made arrangements to fly Marty back to Arizona where he'd stay with Nadine until we returned.

Gary and Philip went to pick up the shiny new RV while Mitch and I started closing up the house. We had invited Candy and Nadine to come along, but neither felt up to such a long trip away from home. We let the kids know where we'd be for the next two months, and then packed our bags for the true north. I pulled on Carolyn's sweater, placed Thunder and Rocket in each of the pockets and closed the door behind me, ready for our new adventure.

The guys shared the driving while I made lists of all the food, clothing and emergency supplies we'd need to pick up along the way. Using a directory and the internet, Mitch and I were able to map out where to refuel and camp overnight in the U.S. and Canada.

About one week after we left, the news reports started. Our Norwegian hero's act of love rekindled the right to die and euthanasia controversies that simmered under the surface of a country gone wild over the Parental Certification Program.

Doug's case was plastered on the news nationwide. There were advocates who supported his actions; others called him a cold blooded murderer. Families cried out about the need for changes in the law; others more intimate with euthanasia remained silent not wanting to attract attention.

Gary's idea to get out of town was wise indeed. Traveling on the road allowed us to escape the controversy. While we were gone, Candy did occasional patrols and Nadine collected our mail. Whenever we planned to stay in one spot longer than five days, Nadine shipped our mail up to the town's post office.

Mitch and I ate peanut butter and jelly sandwiches, smoked our daily weed and giggled in the back of the RV like a couple of kids on a school bus.

When Mitch was driving, Gary would ride shotgun while Philip and I would play cards. When Philip drove, Mitch would ride shotgun while Gary and I fixed a meal.

Riding shotgun was important: it was that person's responsibility to scan the road for wildlife or hazardous traffic. That was not a job for me due to having only one eye, so I spent most of the time perched in between the driver and passenger or sitting in the back near large picture windows.

At times I felt like a galley slave, but I quickly turned this around instead to feeling like a Queen, being driven by her knights in shining armor, the senior contingent.

Having Thunder and Rocket along brought us comfort, hoping they'd be good noise makers to warn us of animals lurking near the RV during the night. We perched them in a windowsill above the kitchen sink.

It wasn't long before we got into bear country where we saw big sky, big moose and big buffalo. We glided along the highway like a freight train through Montana escorted by antelope, elk and deer that seemed to dance all around us.

After crossing into Alberta, Canada we smelled smoke from a wild fire up ahead that waylaid us until morning. We spent time in Banff and then moved north along the Icefields Parkway to Jasper National Park.

It was good to see the sights again, pointing out to Mitch and Philip all the places Gary and I had visited before.

We saw a blonde grizzly in the distance searching for his morning meal and watched as he stood up to sniff the air. Another large brown grizzly lumbered across the road in front of the RV and we gave him a wide berth.

A bull moose, with a seven foot wide rack, galloped like a horse through a far-away field growing impatient I'm sure for the annual rut.

We traveled farther north into the Northwest Territories, and saw distant mountains and rolling hills, drank coffee under pink and purple sunrises and ate dinner under crimson skies in dark surroundings when the only light visible came from our camp fire and the billions of stars overhead.

Mitch impressed us with his knowledge of everything wild and cold and soon became our personal tour guide. He read to us nightly from one of his collections about the gold rush of 1898.

On our travels we visited the towns of White Horse, Carmacks and Dawson City and learned the history of places like Fortymile, Circle City, Bonanza Creek and Eldorado. We learned about dirt poor cheechakoes, hearty sourdoughs and starving miners who became millionaires overnight.

He showed us on the map where boats and equipment were hauled up over snow covered mountains, assembled on the other side and paddled up the Yukon River in the spring. Men with fancy nicknames, who like countless others, risked everything for their chance to dig deep into frozen terrain with a pick axe and shovel in search of gold.

We visited wildlife sanctuaries, observed eagles, hawks and other raptors sail overhead and watched the dancing quivering lights of the aurora at night, lighting up the sky in mysterious colors of jade green, crimson and pale yellow.

Our conversations would've seemed dull to strangers, but silence is abundant when people are content to sit beside each other on a boulder or a log; seizing the warmth of a hot cup of tea to stave off the chill in their bones.

We talked about everything – except the painful recent past.

We talked about the weather and how snow was a good insulator; how one could die of hypothermia in rain and wind just as soon as they would in freezing weather.

With headlamps beaming from our foreheads we read to each other beside the golden radiance of snapping fires while resting in primitive seats burrowed into the earth.

173

We watched eagerly as the moon rose into an ethereal sky each night casting bright light onto the surrounding silhouette of high rolling ridgelines.

We often felt a peculiar paranoia that off in the distance there were eyes resting on us that we could not see. As we watched the moon, we heard the cries of wolves calling out to their young ones as if to say, "It's getting dark – I want you home in an hour." We could hear their wide paws pounding the dirt packed ground as they loped through the brush nearby while keeping a safe distance.

Thunder and Rocket were silent, trembling inside my sweater pockets, rolled up tightly like cinnamon buns. Our Alaskan friends laughed after learning they were our early warning system for approaching grizzlies; Thunder and Rocket being smaller than the Great Alaskan Chipmunk.

We were living in the present surrounded by an abundance of love, beauty and nature. And as the days rolled on it became clear to each of us that a divine intervention was driving this plan. And if that's so, I certainly got more than I bargained for, when all I wanted to do was dance.

Sitting in my make shift earth chair beats waiting for my boiled eggs over rice, bingo and ice cream at 2., among tangled bodies and broken spirits.

The weather cooled and we arrived in the City of Fairbanks in the middle of the night under a light snowfall. It reminded me of the City of Oz at the edge of the wilderness, but instead of rainbows a low level aurora greeted us in spooky shades of green.

We completed this leg of the trip just in time to replace four shredded tires strapped to the roof, remove a rock imbedded in the shattered windshield and pry away a collection of crushed bugs, dead birds and one dead chipmunk all jammed into the front grill.

Philip had refused to use mosquito spray back at Fort Nelson and had plenty of lingering infected bug bites to show for it. One of his ears itched intensely and was swollen to twice its normal size.

Gary's hemorrhoid started acting up from sitting too long during the drive and I was suffering from a bit of anxiety, fixated on the fact that the further north we went, the longer the drive home would be.

The concept of home occupied my mind for days. Home had been many places for me throughout the years, intangible and elusive, yet always present and moving like a shadow that never took hold. Tom searched long and hard for the utopian place to become the quintessential country doctor and I went along for the ride, like a co-conspirator putting my stock into his happiness. We traveled from California, to Pennsylvania, to New York; then to Minnesota, in search of something he never found and to discover later it was something he never truly wanted.

Now here I was three years after selling our home, living in an elegant RV off a two lane road somewhere south of Fairbanks in the Alaskan wilderness on a pristine mountain lake. The senior contingents of my knights in shining armor were keeping me safe and happy. They are concerned about my welfare. We are concerned about each other.

One crisp September morning, Gary decided to take us on a flight seeing trip circling the summit of Denali, 'The High One', Mt. McKinley. And, as if by Providence, we found ourselves in the right place at the right time once again.

The sky was a stunning cobalt blue and the great white rock glowed in the distance under a morning sun, naked to the outside world.

To savor its beauty free from the tumultuous miasma, is a rare occurrence as the mountain is famous for creating its own weather systems - nature's way of telling us to keep off the grass.

Our plane climbed above the 20,000 foot rock and then circled its ice covered summit. Approaching our target we flew over huge snow-capped crags, long milky colored glaciers sprinkled with silt as if crumbled chocolate cookies had fallen from the sky.

We passed over the occasional dark cylindrical crevasse and observed chunks of ice larger than skyscrapers thrown carelessly about by powerful avalanches.

A group of mountain climbers trekked upward upon the surface of the Muldrow Glacier to fulfill a risky, but admirable ambition. The providential return to tell their tale to the armchair adventurers seated in their leather chairs in front of warm fireplaces. How else would people know the power behind the swing of an ice axe, the smell of blue ice and fresh fallen snow, and the colors of an awakening day, the boom of an oncoming avalanche or the force of a relentless wind? All of this would be concealed from the world if climbers never took the chance stretching their hamstrings to the max.

Our flight continued and hit downdrafts dipping us as much as 50 feet at times breaking the hypnotic trance. Each time it happened, I yelped a loud, "HEY!" in the direction of the pilot, as if that would make a difference. Gary, sitting behind me, placed his hands on my shoulders reassuringly, yet I waited for him to vomit in my direction at any moment. Thankfully, that never happened. Philip's face had a look of concern and Mitch handed me a note asking where the parachutes were stashed.

So while I was grateful to see Denali up close and personal, I was thankful our flight was cut short by a weather system churning down from the northwest. I quietly said a heartfelt 'Good-bye' to a beauty I'd never see again.

We landed back onto a quieted still earth, each of us saying little while trying to shake off the after effects of the roller coaster ride. We wanted to shout out to everyone, telling them we had just circled 'The High One'. But all we did was get high ourselves with a good stiff drink and a hot meal. With winter fast approaching the North Country, we decided to begin the trek back home to Arizona.

Two days later over dinner, we looked out over a roaring, silt laden Yukon River and Philip wondered aloud if he had made the right choice not to go to Canada so long ago. Then, to our surprise, he began talking about Vietnam as if it all took place yesterday. Perhaps it was the strength and spirit of the Yukon giving him courage to break the long held silence.

He started off by telling us he never met any mountain climbers in Vietnam; that most of the guys he met were from small town America; places named Levittown, Lincoln, Maple Corners and Bethlehem. They were the sons of farmers, carpenters and mechanics; graduates of tech school. And despite what was told to the American public, most had never graduated from high school. These young men didn't talk about their dreams of the future; they focused on surviving the night.

"You never told us why you changed your mind - why you decided not to go to Canada," I asked.

"I wish I could say it was something romantic, like the love of a beautiful woman. But instead, I was living in the woods with a bunch of guys I hooked up with in Vermont. There was lots of talk and anger about the war to the point where I couldn't hear myself think. So I took my gear and hiked up a large hill overlooking a lake to spend the night alone. The next morning I awakened to a stunning scene where patches of fog hung in between emerald green hills."

"The mountains were steep and I remember that it was very quiet. I heard nothing except a couple of blue jays fighting nearby. The entire panorama could've been taken right out of Vietnam, absent the humidity and jungle. I thought about the people of Vietnam – what they must have been going through."

"And then I went down to a corner store for some breakfast. There I met a grief stricken middle aged couple who had lost their only son who'd enlisted in the Army against their wishes. I think they knew what I was up to.

"They knew I wasn't from their neck of the woods and could tell I had a lot on my mind - I wasn't the first draft dodger they'd seen pass through town. They understood the protests and the way people were feeling about the war, but believed that regardless of the politics, peace anywhere in the world was worth fighting for. They asked me how I'd feel if it was our country being invaded."

"They wanted their son's death to have meaning and showed me a point of view I hadn't thought about before."

"By the time we were done talking, I was ashamed of myself. So I headed over to New York to say good-bye to my parents and then reported for duty knowing full well I could never live with myself if I had followed through with my plans. I was damned if I do and damned if I didn't and would've been miserable either way, so I made the decision to go. I was so scared I acquired a stutter by the time I reached my parents' house."

"Well, maybe if you would've kept it up, they would've found you unfit for duty," I said.

"Oh hell, they were taking anybody and everybody," he added. "Some kids over there didn't know how to read."

"They didn't take me…said I was too ugly," Mitch admitted adding some levity.

"Ok - well I can understand that," Philip responded jokingly. "You have to look good in the uniform."

We left the Yukon the next day traveling the same route home and touched Arizona soil one month later. The trip had been restorative for us all, most especially for Philip.

15

Our day to day lives continued as before, all of us taking care of each other, making changes to the ranch as needed. We managed to spend just two more visits at Gary's mountain retreat in California before he decided to let go of this special place. We decided to spend our summers in Arizona cranking down the air conditioner, sipping gin and tonics and frozen daiquiris poolside at mid-day.

And while beautiful, we tired of Marty's repeated versions of Bach and Mozart on the piano reverberating throughout the ranch every day. Mitch's, "don't knock it till you try it" approach worked and soon we were listening to Marty play songs by contemporary artists much closer to our hearts, minds and generation.

Not long after, Nadine moved in. She felt unsafe sleeping alone in her house and it became more practical for her to join us since she and Philip were spending all their time together. She came with fabulous memorabilia to add to our hippie wall of fame.

Our favorite was the original program distributed during the march on Washington when Martin Luther King made his 'I Have a Dream' speech. There were also autographed 45 rpm records by music artists and one music album by a famous jazz musician. We had great fun going through her possessions and learned she had once been a Go-Go dancer appearing on a popular television show.

In time we had a new portrait taken of us all entitled, "The Wrinkle Ranch: the next generation". Gary continued to keep up with all the financial and legal maneuvering keeping us all protected and secure.

Candy was spending a lot of time with Mitch, but never moved into the ranch as she felt safe in her house. Over the years, she managed to accumulate a pretty serious gun collection that she was trained and prepared to use if necessary. We all felt safer when Candy was around.

Every day I checked the newspaper for reports of a silver haired jack booted woman who managed to knock down a home invasion before police arrived, but I never found such a report.

Our son John got his license to practice architecture and was learning the business end of things from Philip. His house in Malibu was nearing completion and his life seemed to be going in a good direction. He was happy and our talks were productive, no longer being driven by his need for power and control over me.

All in all, we were happy and living the good life under the golden glow of the Arizona sunshine.

Then one quiet Sunday morning, as we were eating breakfast outside on the lanai, the dogs barked.

Philip motioned to us to continue eating while he volunteered to see what the dogs were fussing about. He returned a long fifteen minutes later, moments before Gary was heading out to check on him.

"You're not going to believe this," Philip said.

"Oh sure we will. Let us have it right between the eyes," Mitch replied.

"It's Gabrielle."

We looked up in disbelief and put down our forks in unison, the morning ambiance fractured once again.

"So who does she look like?" Mitch asked Philip.

Philip was never good at hiding emotions and we could easily see when his blood pressure was rising.

We watched as his face slowly turned from a pasty pale white to a flushed cherry red; eyes watering as he sat back down in his seat.

"I think I just saw a ghost," he told us.

We all knew at once what that meant.

It was as if Sumana herself returned to us, circa 1966.

Gabrielle was strikingly beautiful and had all of her mother's features; dark hair and eyes, skin the color of chocolate macchiato. She was the only child born to Doug and Sumana and had not seen her parents since 1987.

After all that time, it turned out she was living nearby in New Mexico, just 100 miles east of the Arizona/New Mexico border. And now here she was all alone, her mother gone, her father in prison.

"I received a letter from the government saying this was my parents' last known address," Gabrielle explained.

"Yes, we're familiar with those letters," Gary replied.

"I know that my father is in prison for killing my mother. I watched the news stories," Gabrielle explained further.

"So, if you know they're not here, why did you come?" I asked unsure about my feelings toward her.

"I was hoping to take my mother's art work back to New Mexico with me. Painting was something we did together when I was a child. It would help me feel closer to her if I could have her paintings nearby."

"What do you do for work Gabrielle?" Gary asked.

"Well, I haven't worked a regular job in several years. I've been selling my own artwork to make ends meet."

"Before that I worked at odd jobs in hotels, cleaning rooms and washing dishes," she replied.

"Do you intend to sell your mother's art work to make ends meet?" asked Gary as the inquisition continued.

"No. I intend to display them in my apartment. I'd never sell my mother's paintings."

"Do you live there with your husband?"

"For now I'm by myself until he gets paroled," replied Gabrielle who shifted in the chair and tapped her foot nervously.

"What's he in jail for?"

"Drugs. But he's clean now. We're both clean," she added shaking her head up and down with a bit of hesitation in her voice. "I go to the methadone clinic now."

"You know Gabrielle, when we all decided to live here together, we agreed to share everything. All of our possessions belong to a trust, including your mother's paintings. They'll belong to the Wrinkle Ranch, even after we're gone," Philip added.

"Have you been to visit your dad?" Mitch asked.

"I went to visit him yesterday, but they said he was in the infirmary and on his way to a local hospital. He's sick - something about his kidneys."

"Your dad would be the only one who could change the trust at this time, Gabrielle. I'll go visit your dad and ask if he is willing to give up your mother's paintings and I'll let you know what he says," Gary said trying to wrap up the discussion.

Gabrielle left us her contact information and sailed through the door less than 45 minutes after she arrived.

We had to hand it once again to Gary, for cutting to the chase and sizing her up so quickly.

"I'll make the trip to visit Doug, but it's unlikely any of Sumana's paintings will be going to Gabrielle and her husband," remarked Gary.

"But Doug gave us strict orders not to visit," Mitch reminded.

"They'll let me in," Gary replied with certainty.

"I'm his estate planning attorney who's concerned about his health. Kidney failure might make a good case for parole and they'll need a place to send him. They'd be stupid not to let me in," reasoned Gary.

"Do you think that's really possible?" asked Philip. "Maybe we should talk about this."

"I guess I wouldn't mind. Didn't we take some sort of vow, until death, do we part or something? I don't mind if he came home, but he's not touching my food," Mitch yelped.

"Well hell, he's not touching my vitamins either," cried a nervous Philip.

"Living with a murderer; now that's something I thought I'd never do," remarked Nadine. "My father would roll back over in his grave."

"Why did he roll over the first time?" asked Philip.

"For moving in with a white man," replied Nadine.

"Yeah, but don't I get Veteran's points?" Philip smiled.

"Doug is sick and needs our help," I reminded everyone.

"Just so you know, if he asks me to kill him, I won't do it," added Mitch. "I don't need that hassle."

"This house belongs to Doug as much as it belongs to each of us. And if he's sick, we'll take care of him, like we promised," Gary stated. "Besides, there's no place he could go – nursing homes and group homes are full. There's no room at the inn."

"I didn't get the chance to know Doug. Does he like music?" asked Marty.

"Doug loves music!" Mitch said.

"That's good to know," added Marty.

"What if he doesn't want to come here?" I asked.

"He'll have no choice. A Judge would need to order it and we'd need to demonstrate we could care for him," added Gary. "I think we can do that."

"I'm not so sure we can. Even with two nurses, we failed Sumana," I added. "We failed to protect her."

"We didn't fail Sumana. She was well taken care of. It was Doug who chose to take her life. We couldn't protect her because we had no way of knowing his plan," reasoned Mitch.

"We couldn't protect her from the flaw in Doug's character," stated Philip.

"Depending on your view of euthanasia, it wasn't the flaw in his character we missed, it was the strength of his character we didn't know he had," Nadine stated eloquently.

The debate over euthanasia resurfaced inside our living room that night. Was Doug right or wrong? Did we fail to protect Sumana? Would Doug take another life? Could we ever do what Doug did for Sumana?

Marty and Nadine were less passionate about the discussion and interjected much needed wisdom from time to time. Finally Marty asked us, "What is it about Doug that you lost when he went away, that you'll regain again when he returns?"

This helped each of us to think about Doug in a different perspective. We talked about his love of music, his humor, our memories and most of all, Sumana. Perhaps if we can be close to Doug in proximity, we can feel close once again to Sumana.

Marty looked up and asked, "Didn't one of you say he was Jewish?"

"No. When we first met Doug he had been planning on converting to Judaism. I remember he took some classes in college to learn more about the history of Israel," I added.

"Maybe I can help him convert," Marty concluded. "It's never too late you know."

"Maybe you can," I said.

So the die was cast. Gary was going to make the necessary arrangements for Doug to come home.

Gary met with the prison officials about Doug's health and just as he outlined the plan to us, the officials agreed to bring the matter before a Judge.

I accompanied Gary for his first meeting with Doug and discovered that what Gabrielle reported was true. Doug was suffering from kidney failure and required dialysis weekly, a treatment not provided by the contractor paid to provide prisoner health care.

Dialysis required repeated trips to the hospital 60 miles away and prison authorities were searching for an alternative living arrangement for Doug, but without much luck.

"We had a visitor the other day," Gary said talking to Doug.

"She came here too, but I was on my way to the hospital," Doug replied.

"She knows what happened and followed the news reports."

"How'd she look?" asked Doug.

"Good. She looked healthy," replied Gary, saying nothing about her resemblance to Sumana.

"Was he with her?"

"No. He's in prison for drug use - that's all I know," Gary said. "She lives in New Mexico – 100 miles east of the Arizona/New Mexico border."

Doug dropped his head low inside the palm of both hands and began sobbing as if revisiting all the anguish Gabrielle had caused him and Sumana years ago.

"Does she have any children?" Doug asked.

"She didn't say," Gary replied suddenly feeling bad for not having asked her.

"Doug, we didn't come here today to discuss Gabrielle. We came to talk about your health," Gary said cutting to the chase.

"Gonna' give me one of your kidneys or something?" Doug asked.

"The prison needs to cut you loose so you can get adequate health care. They're willing to ask a Judge to grant you parole and allow you to return home to live with us. You'd have a parole officer who'd check on you weekly," Gary added.

"You mean go back to the Wrinkle Ranch?"

"Yeah, so we can take care of you," Gary concluded. "There'd be a court hearing and it would need to be ordered by a Judge," he added.

"You're kind of quiet Sharon," Doug said looking at me.

"I want you to come home Doug. All is forgiven and in the past. We need to move forward with living and I want you to get the best health care possible," was all I could say.

"Has Philip and Mitch weighed in on this?" Doug asked.

"Everyone is in agreement," replied Gary.

We told Doug about our trip to Alaska and that Marty and Nadine had moved in with us, that Mitch was still involved with Candy and that he had reconnected with his boys.

"Well, I guess it's better than a sharp stick in the eye," Doug said. "When is all this going to happen?"

"The court hearing is scheduled next week. It's funny how the wheels of justice move faster when cost becomes the issue," said Gary.

"I'll start working on finding some private duty nurses to help pick up the slack," I added.

"What about the two that took care of Sumana?" Doug asked.

187

"They're already booked," I said not wanting to tell him the truth; that they refused to care for him because of what he did to Sumana.

"There's just one other item Doug. Gabrielle asked for Sumana's paintings. I'm supposed to give her an answer," relayed Gary.

"Why would I give away Sumana's paintings?"

"Gabrielle said they'd make her feel closer to Sumana; that as a child Sumana and her used to paint all the time."

"Gabrielle had an opportunity to be close to both of us and she chose to go away. Even when I'm dead and gone, Gabrielle should never get her hands on Sumana's art pieces – they stay with the Wrinkle Ranch forever," Doug said adamantly.

"I was hoping you'd say that," Gary replied.

16

That night over dinner we discussed cutting loose one of our kidneys.

"Between all of us there are 12 kidneys sitting around the table," I pointed out. "Doug only needs one."

"When we talked about living together, I don't recall any discussion about sharing body parts," said Philip.

"Yeah, well the last time we lived together we shared some body fluids Philip and you didn't seem to mind that," I added looking Philip directly in the eye.

"Who's sharing? We're giving it away permanently," added Mitch. "No backsies."

"I don't have many years left. Maybe he could have one of mine," added Marty.

"I don't think you'd be a candidate because of your age Marty," added Nadine. "The surgery is rough - I know. I gave a kidney to my younger sister when she was 12 years old."

"You never told me you had a younger sister," Philip remarked.

"I meant to, but it is painful to talk about. Her body rejected my kidney and she lived only a few months after the surgery. So, you see, we really only have 11 kidneys around the table. Unfortunately, I would not be a candidate."

"I wonder if I would be a good match, given the cancer treatment and all," Gary asked me.

"I'm not sure," was all I could say.

"So which one of you pussy's is interested in donating their kidney to help Doug stay alive?" I asked looking around the table for volunteers.

Silence engulfed the room.

"I'll do it if the doctors say it is okay," stated Gary.

"I only have one eye. Why not have only one kidney?" I surmised. "I dedicated my life to health care a long time ago – this would just be an extension of that."

"If Doug's body rejects my kidney, can I have it back?" Philip asked me.

"I don't think that's an option," I replied.

"I think I'll sit this one out. I had problems with my kidneys during the days I was using," Mitch said. "I had a lot of infections and suffered from dehydration to the point I was hospitalized. Donating a kidney might not be a good idea."

"Gary, we have so much money, can't we just buy one?" asked Philip.

"I wonder how much they cost. We should have a kidney store around here somewhere –where's the phone book?"

With Mitch, Nadine and Marty out of the running and Philip reluctant to nut up, that left just Gary and me. In the days that followed I did research into the trials and tribulations of donating a kidney while Gary prepared to make a case to the Judge to care for Doug and assure the Parole Board we'd keep Doug on the straight and narrow.

In a letter to Gabrielle, Gary informed her she would not be receiving any of Sumana's art work; that Doug had refused her request even in the event of his death. In the letter Gary added that Doug would be coming back to the Wrinkle Ranch should she need this information to file her Parental Certification form with the federal government.

That was the end of the matter, until six months later, when Doug's kidneys began to fail which prompted an unexpected turn of events.

Once again the misanthropist in me raised her ugly head. We talked about the Parental Certification Program and the pain it caused - the chaos merciless. The news reports continued, the shortages were protracted and care for our nation's elderly suffered from a perpetual case of lockjaw; stories plentiful about lives uprooted, displaced elderly and families gone haywire or bankrupt in their attempts to fulfill a mandated obligation.

New situations arose where the parents were 102 years old with children in their eighties and grandchildren in their sixties. Who's taking care of whom?

The naïve believed the success stories, while the savvy knew that success came with a price tag – updated trusts, wills and jointly held bank accounts. Exploitation was rampant. You never heard about children giving mom a much needed kidney or helping dad with a life-saving bone marrow transplant.

But in my heart I knew those families existed – the ones who cared for their loved ones with devotion in their own homes or from a distance, but never bragged about it.

It was certainly a blessing that Mitch was reunited with his family, but we worried that in the event of failing health, at some not too far off distant future, they'd challenge our ability to care for him and steal him away to the east coast.

During the final stretch, Mitch and Philip finally acquiesced to donating one of their kidneys. But as it turned out none of us was a good match for one reason or another. And when that happened, Doug's name was placed on a list.

The long months of waiting were taxing. The days between dialysis shortened and Doug grew weak. His doctors made one final plea to enlist Gabrielle before Doug lapsed into unconsciousness forever.

With no time to waste, Gary, Philip and Mitch drove to New Mexico to bring Gabrielle back to Arizona to save her father's life.

When Philip knocked on the door, they heard a man's voice.

"Who's there?" he asked.

"You don't know us. We're here to talk with Gabrielle," replied Philip.

"She's not here," said the voice.

"Can you tell us where we can find her?" asked Mitch.

"No."

"Look, it's pretty important. Her father is sick and we need to talk with her right away," Gary said.

"She's not here – left over a week ago."

"Can you tell us where she's working?" asked Mitch.

"No. She went to live with a friend across town," was all the voice would say. "If you find her, tell her she left her address book here in a box with some other things."

Gary and Mitch looked at one another.

"Just give us the box. We'll make sure she gets her stuff," Gary added.

The man opened the door allowing them to enter and pointed to a dark corner on the opposite side of the room.

The apartment was small and smelled of warm beer. Gary walked over to the man and handed him a business card.

"Have her call me if she comes by," Gary told the man.

They rifled through the box to find Gabrielle's address book and then split up; Mitch and Gary knocking on doors and Philip making calls. Where had Gabrielle gone? No one had seen her for days.

Nadine, Marty and I stood nearby as the nurse monitored Doug's blood pressure while he gazed at Sumana's paintings. He was weak but continued to eat well and drink fluids. He had a healthy attitude and his sense of humor was intact.

"I almost gave you a kidney," Marty said to Doug. "That would've made you just a little Jewish."

Doug laughed out loud in response.

"Well, if I get out of this alive, promise me you'll help me convert," he added.

"I will. That's a promise," said Marty shaking his finger.

"Have they found Gabrielle yet?" Doug asked.

"No, I don't think so. They would've called," I replied.

"Now I'm worried about her," Doug added. "Maybe she's in trouble and needs my help."

"You two pass like ships in the night. She leaves you and Sumana as a young girl and misses out on a lifetime of memories. Then she lives in a bordering state close in proximity to her dying mother and never knew it. She visits you in prison on the same day and exact time you are scheduled for dialysis miles away at another hospital. Now you need her and you can't find her," Nadine pointed out.

"One of our favorite games when she was a kid was hide and seek. I guess we've been playing it our whole lives. Maybe it's too late now. Maybe she's really gone forever."

"It's never too late Doug. After WWII people were separated for decades from their loved ones, only to reunite when they least expected it. I've seen amazing things happen in my life. Always hope for the best," added Marty.

With not much else to say, we sat there quietly waiting for a call, when all of a sudden…the dogs barked.

I could've had two orgasms by the time Nadine reached the front door – her inexhaustible shuffle driving me mad.

Nadine opened the front door to find a tearful Gabrielle standing in the heat of the day beside a dirt encrusted truck loaded with luggage and boxes. She was not alone.

Standing by her side dressed in his Sunday best, was a young boy, aged 10 or 11, with blonde hair parted down the middle that rested tastefully just behind each ear. The young boy named Raj was her son.

Gabrielle had finally come home.

One of the most beautiful times of my life took place when my friends and I lived under one roof. Some people called it a commune, but we called it 'The Wrinkle Ranch'. It was an old suburban stucco located just west of Tucson, Arizona that we converted into a beautiful home, lavishly furnished and decorated with love. We lived there rent free in exchange for a promise of unconditional love and commitment. That was the deal.

For all of us, this was a time of transition, from a period when people were preoccupied with status and being told how to live, while feeling a constant pull of how they wanted to live.

While sharing what we had, each bringing our own possessions, skills and resources, we took care of each other and created memories to last a lifetime.

It was a time of yearning, when some of us were estranged and searching for a home. It was a time of understanding, to know and accept people outside of our traditional and often times isolated families. Where there was pain, we infused love. Where there was uncertainty, we added hope.

During those years we learned once again about the meaning of love, compassion and sustenance. We learned, through patience and tolerance, about people different from ourselves in culture, thoughts, and personalities; that everyone should be accepted and respected for who they were. There was no grandiosity. No one individual had the answer for everything.

As children growing up we all watched the same television shows and naively believed that everyone lived in pretty houses overflowing with a loving family, doing chores without complaining. This is what we had in mind, I think, when we met at Carolyn's house in search of peace and love; something we could call our own.

I'd like to think that the time we spent together helped set the tone for how we lived our future lives. Perhaps I held a utopian view of those years, but I do believe that in one brief span of time, we thrived in peaceful surroundings while existing in a much larger tumultuous world. For a few, it turned out to be the only peace they had ever known.

We continue our lives here at The Wrinkle Ranch, under the glow of the Arizona sunshine, each day filled with love and the promise that we'll be there for each other until death do we part. Each of us know that we're in good hands, surrounded by strength of character, a dash of human kindness, unconditional love, commitment and caring - the same ingredients that baked that magic so long ago.

Before putting down my pen, I do my nightly rounds. The nurse was sent home – her services no longer needed until some future point in time. Doug, Gabrielle and Raj are in the living room looking at family photographs.

Gary is asleep in his recliner; a book about Mount Everest resting on his chest. Marty was playing soft somber tunes on his piano savoring a tumbler of scotch. Philip and Nadine were watching a 1940's black and white movie, smoking their medicinal weed, eating cookies and popcorn. Mitch and Candy were on the phone with their New York literary agent arguing over language in a contract.

On this night, I kept the frenzied world at bay – silenced the misanthropist within and chose instead to live in a world of peace; my faith in humanity restored.

Some say that you can never go home again. I did… and it worked out just fine.

And just as I put down my pen….the dogs barked.

Epilogue

After losing her vision completely, Sharon continued to live at the Wrinkle Ranch for another nine years. She passed away peacefully in the arms of her knights in shining armor and joined Carolyn, Jackson, Sumana and Marty, along with his wife, in the Solitude Room.

Gary was the next to go. From what we could tell, he died from a broken heart, having lost the only true love of his life.

Philip suffered two cardiac events, but it was the third that finally took him. He died while the heart replacement he paid for was in transit. The heart was given later that same day to a young Vietnamese woman in New York. Philip wouldn't have wanted it any other way. His service, complete with full military honors made his son John proud.

Mitch was stricken with pancreatic cancer. His battle was a short one, but he lived to see his memoir published. There were many family members in attendance at his funeral, including his wife Candy and a brother we never knew he had.

Nadine contracted a virus and died of a stroke a few weeks later. As she wished, we laid her to rest next to the Colonel in the family mausoleum in Georgia.

I won the tontine: a 100 year old bottle of Scotch, a single shot glass and a photo of us on the porch at Peaceful. I toasted my beautiful wife, my family and my friends, laughed until I cried and danced naked in the solitude room. The Wrinkle Ranch lives on....and with the death of a thousand cuts.....so do I.

Shalom, Doug

Made in the USA
Middletown, DE
22 May 2015